Dog Star Night

A Fantasy Adventure

Kenneth James

Dogstarnight, LLC
Williamsburg, Virginia

For information, address llcdogstar@gmail.com

First edition

Designed by Evan Shapiro, Green Avenue Design

Illustrated by Melissa Whitaker

979-8-9856082-0-5 Paperback

979-8-9856082-1-2 Hardback

For John Ryan

CONTENTS

PROLOGUE

Mountain shadows stretched across the valley toward where Chieftain Orion stood on a rocky outcrop. A young mother approached him. She raised her newborn baby boy up above her head. Orion scooped the infant into his giant right hand and lifted the child toward the setting Sun. The child was the first to be born into Orion's tribe since the onset of the Great Freeze five years ago.

It was a tribal custom for the Chieftain to announce the newborn's name to the Sun. "To you, Eternal Light, and to all those you watch over, I present Benjamin."

Benjamin was an ancient name, rarely given, and then only to one who possessed both wisdom and courage.

A green ray of light flashed across the western horizon, the Sun's acknowledgment of approval.

Orion passed Benjamin to his wife, Beatrix, who quickly applied an herbal ointment to mask the baby's human scent.

CHAPTER 1

Bloody Lip

There was a rare snowfall Friday night in the desert town of Prickly Pear. Benny woke up Saturday morning to find almost five inches of snow covering the rocky ground and cactus around his house. He spent the afternoon making his first snowman. The trickiest part was putting a worn-out cowboy hat on the snowman's head. That feat was accomplished by a balancing act on a wobbly, flipped-over garbage can.

Benny stood back to admire his snow cowboy. The cowboy wore two six-shooters and a vest. The six-shooters were old-fashioned wooden toys from a discarded box in the carport's storage shed. His dad had played with them as a kid. The vest was a frayed pillowcase with faded fighter jets on it.

Such an odd sight, a snow cowboy next to a saguaro cactus!

Benny was thinking about how he might add a sheriff's badge to the vest when, from behind, he heard the taunting baby talk.

"Did widdle Ratboy make a big snowman?"

Benny didn't have to turn around to know it was DJ mocking him. DJ never missed a chance to make fun of the "rat" part of Benny's last name, Tratten. Whatever made DJ a bully must have been contagious, because other neighborhood kids had started calling Benny "Ratboy" too.

"Why don't you put whiskers and a tail on it and make a snowrat?" DJ wasn't letting up.

Benny turned to face DJ and yelled, "Go away. Leave—," but he never finished.

A hard-packed snowball smacked him in the mouth. Benny could taste blood from his split lip, but he felt no pain, only confusion. Why? What did I ever do to him?

The cowboy snowman was DJ's next target. He cackled as he tumbled it to the ground and stomped on it. "I'm making a snow pancake!"

Clearly, DJ was trying to sucker him into a fight. It was a tactic Benny had witnessed before. DJ would torment a kid into reacting, then pound the kid into the ground. After that, DJ would play the poor, innocent victim and plead, "He threw the first punch. I was only protecting myself."

DJ was bigger and stronger. But, most of all, DJ was mean. If Benny reacted, DJ would beat him up and walk away blameless. Benny's only real choice was not to give the bully what he wanted, so he did nothing. He held back. That choice came with a different kind of punch.

Flapping his arms like chicken wings, DJ bobbed around, squawking, "Maybe tomorrow you can make a snow chicken. Cluck. Cluck. Cluck."

If Benny had a superpower, he'd want it to be invisibility. Then, he could vanish into thin air and hide from his helplessness.

DJ picked up the six-shooters. "These are cool. I'll keep 'em."

Benny didn't hear a word DJ was saying. He was fixated on a thought—hide, and the bully wins.

"I'll take this too." DJ put on the cowboy hat and strutted off, still clucking, "Look! I'm a chicken cowboy."

Now, instead of invisibility, Benny wanted the power to vaporize DJ into a million harmless particles, to make DJ be the one to disappear.

As he knelt next to his flattened snowman, Benny shook with anger, trying not to cry. None of this would have happened if his old dog, Max, were still around. DJ was afraid of Max, who would snarl and growl whenever DJ came near. But Max was gone. He'd gone to wherever dogs go when they move on from this world. That was forty-six days ago, three days after Christmas.

Benny had counted the days. His parents told him that, as time passed, he wouldn't miss Max so much. Of this, Benny was now certain—forty-six days wasn't enough time. He missed Max today more than ever. He could no longer hold back the tears.

Behind him, there was a childish cry. "Wahhh-wahhh." Benny resisted turning his head, fearing a second snowball to the face. He was sure DJ had come back and was now teasing him for crying.

The cry repeated. "Wahhh-wahhh. Ouch-ouch." This time the voice sounded like his little sister, Dyna. Panic swept through him. Had DJ hurt Dyna too? Benny sprung to his feet. Clenching his fists to shield his face, he spun around to confront … no one. At least, no one at eye level.

Yet another "Wahhh-wahhh" sounded from the ground by his feet. Benny looked down to see the strangest looking dog he'd ever seen staring back up at him. The dog was long and squatty, with big floppy ears and folds of droopy skin on its neck and shoulders. Its fur was a combination of bright rainbow colors that simply didn't belong on a dog. Most curious, the dog had a big hump on its back that made it look like a short-legged camel.

"Why-why. Cry-cry. Ouch-ouch?" There was no doubt this came from the camel dog, but its mouth hadn't moved. And there was no mistaking the tone. The dog was inquiring about Benny and sounded concerned.

To put the dog at ease, Benny decided to reply, "I'm okay, no ouch-ouch. I'm not hurt. I'm mad."

Then, curiosity overtook him. "How can you talk? Why don't you move your lips? Where is—" He stopped himself, feeling foolish. It had to be some kind of trick.

Benny suspected DJ and his buddies were listening and laughing. "I know it's you, DJ. You didn't fool me. I know you hid a walkie-talkie." All the kids in DJ's group played army commando in the desert behind the houses, and a few of the kids had military-style walkie-talkies.

"It's so obvious, DJ. You hid the walkie-talkie in the dog's hump." Benny said this loudly and clearly, directing his voice at the hump.

The response to this was beyond incredible. The camel hump started wiggling and a head popped out. A puppy had been blanketed in the loose folds of fur on the bigger dog's back. The puppy spoke. "Bella-Bella, walk-walk. Pup-Pup, talk-talk."

Benny caught his jaw dropping just enough to ask the passenger puppy, "Are those your names? Are you Pup? Is the rainbow dog Bella?"

The puppy jumped down and looked up. "Bella-Bella, yep-yep. Pup-Pup, yup-yup."

Still not believing his ears, Benny asked, "Where'd you learn to talk?"

"Star-star, far-far," Pup replied.

Benny was about to ask why Pup talked in double words and rhymes, when Mom called out from the front door, "Time for dinner."

"My mom's calling me. I gotta go. You'd better go home too. It's getting cold and it's going to be freezing tonight. You should come back tomorrow, so we can play in the snow. Can you?"

Pup casually flipped his head sideways and scratched his left ear, giving the impression he hadn't heard a word Benny had said.

Benny repeated in a louder voice, "Don't forget. Come back if you can."

Mom called again, this time more insistent. "Did you hear me? It's dinner time."

"Coming, Mom."

Upon reaching the door, Mom asked, confused, "Whose dogs are those?"

Benny glanced back to see the pair gazing innocently up at him. The dogs had followed him.

"I don't know. They just wandered up to me. I told them to go home. They don't listen very well."

Mom bent down and examined the dogs.

"They don't have any collars or tags. They're well fed, so they must have an owner. What's all that colored dust on them? What an odd pair."

"You're not gonna believe this, Mom. Pup can talk! Not just dog-barking like 'woof-woof and arf-arf,' but real people-words."

Benny turned to Pup. "Say something! Say 'Talk-talk, walk-walk.' Or 'star-star, far-far.'" But Pup wouldn't say a "word-word," and only barked and romped like a puppy.

Mom laughed. "I believe you. Pup is probably shy around adults."

By her laugh, Benny knew Mom was only humoring him. But, humor or not, she was right—Pup would never talk in front of a grown-up. Even if Pup did, grown-ups wouldn't believe what they heard, anyway.

Just then, Mom's confusion over the dogs turned to concern for her son.

"What happened to your lip? It's bleeding. Are you okay?"

"I'm okay. DJ hit me with a hard snowball." Benny said this in an even voice, trying not to make a big deal out of it.

Mom was angry. "That kid is out of control. It's to the point where I need to have a talk with his mother."

"No, Mom. Don't! It'll only make things worse."

Then, hoping to help the dogs gain entry into the warm house, Benny decided to tell a fib.

"DJ ran off scared, anyway. Bella sneered and growled at him. Her growl is as mean as Max's."

Mom looked down into the gentle brown eyes of the rainbow dog. "I don't think this dog has a mean bone in her body."

Benny finished off his deception with a clincher.

"Bella protected me, so we need to take care of her. We can't leave her and Pup out in the freezing cold tonight."

Mom allowed the dogs to come in. Bella's eyes, not Benny's fib, were the key to entry.

CHAPTER 2

The Sword Handle

All the commotion at the front door brought Benny's dad and sister, Dyna, into the room from the kitchen. The dogs raised their noses to catch the smells of onions, pepper, and grilled beef that followed them.

Dad was perplexed. "What the heck is going on here?"

Mom stated the dogs' case before Dad could say anything more. "The dogs wandered up to Benny. We can't leave them outside tonight. It's supposed to drop into the teens. That's dangerously cold."

"We can't just take in every stray animal wandering the neighborhood," Dad countered. "We know nothing about these dogs. They could have rabies."

Mom was determined. "These dogs don't have rabies. They obviously have an owner. They're perfectly well fed, just dusty. I'm not leaving them out tonight to die of exposure."

Dad had no choice but to say yes. That "Yes" came with a stern stipulation.

"Benny, we won't be keeping these dogs. If we can't find their owner tomorrow, we'll have to take them to the animal shelter when it opens Monday morning. Do you understand?"

Benny hesitated because the right answer was not a simple "yes" or "no."

What Benny understood was that Dad was against *ever* getting a new dog. Benny's twelfth birthday was coming up soon, and he'd twice asked for a new puppy as a present. The first time Dad had dismissed Benny with a flat "No." The second time Dad responded with "No, and don't ask again."

Benny knew what was behind Dad's terse refusal. It was because of that terrible morning forty-six days ago. Like he'd done every morning, Benny had nudged Max, who always slept in bed next to him, to wake up and start the day. But that morning, Max didn't budge. His eyes didn't open. His tail didn't wag. Max lay lifeless. A wrenching pain gripped Benny's stomach and he couldn't breathe. Gasping, Benny finally caught a single breath and yelled, "Dad! Dad!"

In seconds, Dad rushed in to find Benny clinging to Max. Kneeling down next to Benny's bed, Dad held Max, too. Benny had never seen Dad cry before, but now his father was sobbing uncontrollably, "Oh, Maxie, ol' fella. My buddy, ol' pal. True friend. The best dog ever." No dog could ever replace Max.

"Well, are you going to answer me or not?" Hearing Dad's voice, Benny was jolted out of this sad memory and back into the present. "You understand we're not keeping these dogs?"

Benny simply answered "Yes."

Once Dyna realized Bella and Pup would be staying, if only for the night, she jumped up and down, clapping her hands. When she ran up to Bella and hugged her, all kinds of colors flew off Bella's coat and into the air everywhere. Dyna's pink shirt became tie-dyed.

Dad looked at the mess of shimmering colors and said, "I guess we'll have to put dinner on hold. These dogs need a bath."

"I'll vacuum up the dust and go next door to borrow some of Guapo's food," Mom said.

The Castillos, who lived next door, had a big chocolate lab named Guapo. Paco Castillo was Benny's best friend, and Benny spent as much time playing next door with Paco and Guapo as he spent at home. The two families were close, so Mom didn't give a second thought to asking for neighborly help.

As Mom headed out the front door, Dad returned to the kitchen to shut down his cooking operations. Usually, Dad grilled out on the back patio on Saturdays, even on crisp winter evenings. But the freezing cold and snow on the ground made this Saturday an exception.

With dinner on hold, Dad led the way to the bathroom, with Bella following happily behind him. Pup was a different story. When Pup reached the bathroom door, he turned tail to run. With a quick hand, Benny grabbed the fleeing dog by the scruff of the neck and lifted him into the air. Pup wiggled and squirmed, but his escape had lost all its traction. Dyna was last into the bathroom, and once she closed the door, Pup accepted his fate.

Before turning on the faucet, Dad had to remove the cooking pot sitting over the bathtub drain. The tub faucet had a slow leak, and since water in the desert was scarce and expensive, the pot collected each and every drop. Dad had battled the leak on and off for almost a year. He had swapped out the spigot and put in new washers, all to no avail. When he replaced the faucet handles, the leak stopped … for two days. He was too stubborn to call a plumber, so the leak persisted.

Usually, the collected water found its way to the house plants. However, the current collection must've been okay for a dirty dog, as Dad dumped it back into the tub. With that as his starting point, he filled the tub up halfway, another water conservation measure.

Pup was plopped into the bath first. It took Dad almost as much time to wash Pup's two large pointy ears as it did the rest of Pup's body. Pup's ears were triangular. Not the kind of triangle where all the sides are equal, but the one where a skinnier base makes the tip more pointy.

Finished with Pup's head and ears, Dad moved on to Pup's body, which was completely covered with rainbow dust from Bella's fur. As the dust washed away, his real coat was uncovered. Pup was mostly white, but had several large brown and reddish-orange patches. His most prominent patch was right on the nape of his neck where Benny had snatched him into the air. That patch was hourglass-shaped and shaded, so that the hourglass appeared more empty than full.

Pup's most curious marking remained hidden until Dad flipped him over to towel off his belly. There, Pup had a square patch that looked like a stitched-on orange pocket. A droopy "8" stretched across the patch, as if it were taking a snooze on a comfy bed.

"Looks like the Lazy 8 Ranch lost one of its dogies." Dad laughed out loud at his own joke.

Benny never got Dad's jokes, and he didn't get this one, either. Still, Benny laughed along, out of kindness.

After Pup, it was Bella's turn. She hopped right into the tub and loved having the warm water poured on her back and the soap scrubbed into her fur. She seemed to think she was at a spa. Watching the rainbow colors swirl down the drain, Benny was keen to see Bella's true coat revealed. But, as Dad scrubbed and scrubbed, Bella's coloring didn't wash away. If anything, her colorful fur only became brighter.

Dad finally conceded. "These are her natural colors. I've never seen a dog like this."

Dyna offered an explanation. "Maybe she dyes her fur."

Dad was still puzzling over Bella's colors when Mom, back from the Castillos, entered the bathroom.

Dad wanted Mom's opinion. "Have you ever seen colors like this on a dog? Or any animal, for that matter?"

Mom studied the newly bathed Bella. "It's more than just her coloring. Her markings look like stars and planets. That silver mark on her hip resembles a crescent moon. She's a cosmic beauty!"

Benny could definitely make out Saturn's pink and gold rings and Jupiter with its dull red spot. The bright red spot on Bella's right shoulder might be Mars.

But, upon closer inspection of the crescent moon, Benny said, "I think the silver mark looks exactly like a sword handle."

Dad contemplated the mark, examining it from different angles, and agreed with Benny.

"It really does look like a hilt of a sword, and that makes her tail look like a curved blade."

Dad tugged at the handle. This resulted in Bella swishing water in Dad's face with her curved blade.

Dad apologized. "Sorry, Bella."

After the bath, as the water drained out of the tub, Dyna shouted out with glee, "Hurray! Mrs. Bubbles got her colors back. And so did Mr. Juggles."

Mrs. Bubbles and Mr. Juggles were Dyna's made-up names for two of the anti-slip stickers Dad had placed on the bottom of the tub years ago. Mrs. Bubbles was a tropical fish with bulging eyes and bubbles coming out her mouth. Mr. Juggles was an octopus. Dyna named him Mr. Juggles because, once upon a time, eight arms juggled eight colorful beach balls. Now, Mr. Juggles tossed around only three.

Over the years, Mr. Juggles had not only lost five beach balls, he'd lost almost all of his purple color. His stylish red bow tie was missing altogether. Mrs. Bubbles had fared no better. She was a pale shadow of her former splendid yellow- and green-striped self. But Dyna was right. The pair were gloriously rejuvenated! Their colors were never brighter. And it wasn't just Mrs. Bubbles and Mr. Juggles who got their colors back. So did the never-named sea turtle, seahorse, and jellyfish.

All the tub creatures were brighter than new.

Dad pressed his thumb on Mr. Juggles to test if his newfound youth was only skin deep. It wasn't. Dad's thumb remained colorless. Next, Dad grabbed a sponge next to the sink and scoured Mrs. Bubbles, trying to remove her colors. He could not. Her colors were permanent.

"Well, I guess I won't be having to replace these stick-ons," Dad remarked. "They're better than new. I can cross it off my to-do list. Thanks, Bella."

Dad had no sooner thanked Bella than a drop dripped from the faucet. One had gotten away! Dad quickly put the pot back under the spout.

Dinner was delayed by an hour, so Benny was hungry when he and Dyna finally sat down to eat. The guest dogs took up positions underneath the table, still licking their chops from Guapo's food, which they had snarfed down.

Dad and Mom shuttled plastic containers from the refrigerator to the table. When the reheated chili arrived, Benny finally figured out what was for dinner. Dad repurposed the hamburgers he was going to grill outside into chili for the taco salad he prepared inside. The onion and pepper smells Benny detected earlier were ingredients for chili. When it came to chili, the household was divided. Benny had inherited Dad's spicy gene, while Mom and Dyna preferred mild. Dad bridged the divide by making two batches of chili, a hot batch with red peppers and a mild batch with yellow.

After dinner, as Benny was getting ready to wash his face and hands before bed, Dad ambled into the bathroom and picked up the pot from the tub. Its tally was meager, only a few drips. He dumped them onto Benny's head. "There. That will help getcha started, Cowboy." This time Benny didn't laugh.

That night, before going to bed, both Benny and Dyna cuddled with the dogs in Benny's room. Dyna was scratching the back of the puppy's neck, when Pup rolled over and said, "Rub-rub-a-dub-dub, tum-tum."

Dyna's face lit up with excitement. "Benny! Benny! Pup can talk!"

"I know, I know," Benny answered. "Just don't ask him to talk in front of Mom and Dad. He won't do it. He won't talk in front of grown-ups."

Dyna looked at Pup and asked, in a rather insistent voice, "Where did you learn to talk?"

Pup pranced over to the bedroom window, stretched out his two pointy ears, and aimed them at the bright star that had moved close to the moon. When Pup scampered back to Dyna, he rolled over in expectation of a belly rub.

"Pup likes being scratched right on his 'crazy 8,'" Dyna said. Earlier, Dyna must've misheard Dad's "Lazy 8" as "Crazy 8." She didn't get the "doggy joke" either.

As Dyna rubbed Pup's tummy, Benny lightly pinched Bella's big, floppy right ear and massaged it between his thumb and finger. Bella enjoyed her ear massage as much as Pup reveled in his tummy rub. Benny was rubbing a black spot on her ear when his finger passed through it.

"Dyna! Look!" Benny exclaimed with his finger sticking through. "Bella has a hole in her ear."

Dyna came over and examined the ear. She wasn't the least bit surprised. "She must wear big, pierced earrings when she attends balls at her palace. Bella must be a queen!" This answer was silly to Benny, who now looked directly at Pup for a better one.

Pup knew the correct answer and offered it: "Wolf-wolf." Instead of "Wolf-wolf," Benny heard "woof-woof." "Wolf" or "woof," it didn't matter. The answer was nonsense to Benny.

It was around midnight when Mom peeked in the door. All were sleeping. Pup was sound asleep on Dyna's lap, while Benny was curled up against Bella. It was Saturday night, and no school tomorrow, so Mom just let them stay that way.

CHAPTER 3

Bully Holds the High Ground

Benny and Dyna played in their backyard with Bella and Pup all through Sunday morning. The sun was out and the weather was getting warmer, but the snow hadn't yet melted much. Benny made a snowball and tossed it up into the air. He watched in amazement as Bella snatched it out of mid-air and gobbled it down with delight.

He wondered to himself: Wow! How can a dog with such short legs jump so high?! He tested "how high" by making another snowball and throwing it straight up in the air, as high as he could. Bella's leap defied gravity. She sprang at least ten feet in the air, landing as gracefully as a ballerina.

What Benny did next was an impulse. He acted without thinking ahead or understanding why he was doing it.

Benny caught sight of Dyna in the corner of the yard, playing with Pup under a mesquite tree. Together, they had built what Benny knew was a small snowdog, because of the floppy ears and long snout. He teased his sister by throwing a snowball into the tree above her. Benny couldn't throw nearly as far as DJ, who was the star pitcher on the neighborhood baseball team. Still, Benny had excellent aim. His snowball hit the branch right over Dyna's head and snow tumbled down.

"Look!" Benny laughed. "I just made a snowgirl."

Benny could see Dyna's face turning red and he knew she was going to charge at him in anger. "Theresa Nicole, you better not," Benny warned. He called Dyna by her real name, like Dad did when she was about to explode. Dyna charged, but her attack was halted by Bella, who jumped between Dyna and Benny. Bella gave Benny a mild growl, followed by a disapproving frown. Pup gave him a curt "Tsk-tsk, tut-tut."

"I didn't do anything wrong," Benny argued. "I was only having some fun."

Dyna glared at Benny. "You're being a bully just like DJ."

Bella's frown dissolved and she gave Benny a sympathetic nod.

Benny understood what Bella was telling him. "I bullied Dyna because DJ bullied me?"

Bella shook her head. "Yes."

Benny turned to Dyna. "I'm sorry."

Dyna replied by hitting Benny with a soft snowball. "You deserved that!"

Benny agreed. "I did."

After lunch, there was a knock at the front door. It was Paco from next door. Neighborhood kids were sledding down the hill at the end of the street, and Paco came to ask if Benny and Dyna wanted to join them. Before Benny could check with Mom, Bella and Pup darted out the front door and gleefully greeted Paco. It was as if the two dogs were Paco's oldest friends.

Pup immediately rolled over and Paco rubbed the puppy's belly. "Oh yes! This perrito loves this! Right here! Right on his infinity pocket!"

Paco was right and Dad was wrong! Dad's "lazy 8" looked anything but lazy. It had whirled to life, like a spinning top, so fast that it appeared to be standing still. Paco looked up at Benny. "You gotta feel this, the pup vibrates!"

Benny got down on one knee and pressed his hand on the symbol. It was vibrating!

"What the heck do you think he keeps in there?" Benny asked.

"I guess, if it's an infinity pocket," Paco answered, "everything."

By this time, Dyna had come to the door. Seeing Paco rubbing Pup on the tummy, Dyna asked, "Did Pup tell you to 'rub-rub-a-dub-dub tum-tum?'"

Benny answered for Paco. "No. Paco already knew what to do."

Mom gave the kids permission to go to the hill, and it was obvious the two dogs wanted to come along. Mom hesitated to allow this. "Benny, we don't have any of Max's old collars or leashes. We gave them all away."

Paco had a solution. Along with their dog, Guapo, his family also had a calico cat named Gato. "Guapo has extra collars that will fit Bella. Gato has a walking leash that Pup can use. I'll run home and get them." Paco was gone before Mom could answer.

When Paco returned, Benny put Guapo's collar on Bella. Bella's neck was very thick, and the collar had to be set to the last notch. "And I thought Guapo had a big neck," Paco remarked.

Harnessing up Pup wasn't easy. Pup squirmed and resisted. Benny was getting frustrated, so Paco offered to try. Paco got down on one knee and looked Pup in the eyes, "I understand, mi perrito. A dog shouldn't wear a cat leash. Por favor. Only this one time." Pup stood calm and quiet as Paco put on the harness. Paco had a way with animals.

Before heading to the hill, Paco suggested they find a couple of plastic garbage can lids to use for sliding saucers. Almost no one in the desert town owned sleds or saucers, and Paco said the lids made good substitutes. Benny grabbed the lid from the wobbly garbage can from yesterday, and the three kids and two dogs were on their way. However, when they arrived at the hill, they were disappointed. From the sunshine and so many kids sliding down on it, the slope had turned into mud.

This disappointment was still sinking in, when, suddenly, a mudball just missed Benny's head. "Look everybody, it's Ratboy, and he's brought his ratty, bratty baby sister." DJ was standing at the top of the hill with a bunch of his underlings.

One of the kids in DJ's gang mimicked DJ's taunts. "Does a little scaredy rat have a new dog? That prissy dog won't be able to protect you like your mean-ole-ugly dog did."

Just then, DJ noticed Paco, who had stepped out from behind Benny and Bella. "Oh, look. It's Ratboy's ratty buddy." DJ's taunt was followed immediately by a second mudball aimed at Paco's head. Paco shielded his head with the lid he was holding, but mud splattered across the right sleeve of his sweatshirt.

Paco shouted back angrily, "Estupido en la cabeza." The insult was in Spanish, but the "stupid" in "estupido" was clear to all.

DJ grew irate, not because of Paco's insult, but because Paco dared to make it. Wanting to put Paco back in his place, DJ retaliated with his most hateful abuse. "Poco Paco, little brown taco, can't even speak English."

Benny started to yell, "Sticks and stones can break my bones—" but the look on Paco's face caused Benny to stop mid-sentence.

Blood vessels were bulging on Paco's forehead. Benny had never seen Paco so mad. Unlike the mudball, DJ's insult hit its target. Paco was going to attack DJ.

Paco charged up the hill, with DJ still taunting him. "Bring it on, Paco Bell. I wanna hear you cry in Spanish."

Benny yelled, "Dyna. Run home as fast as you can and get Dad!" When Dyna didn't reply, Benny turned around to find her gone. Only Pup was there, and Dyna was not at the other end of the leash.

"Pup, where is she?" Benny exclaimed.

Pup pinched his ears together, so they made the shape of a spear tip. He jabbed the tip toward the hilltop. Dyna had rushed headlong up the hill ahead of Paco and was closing in fast upon DJ.

"Look boys, the little 'ratdoll' wants to play with us!" DJ scoffed.

DJ thrust his right arm out to shove Dyna aside, but Dyna slipped under it and delivered a hard punch to DJ's gut. Dyna wasn't so comical anymore.

Enraged, DJ grabbed Dyna by her hair and tossed her aside like a ragdoll.

Suddenly, there was a blur, or a flash, or both. Benny was waiting for Dyna to come tumbling down the muddy hill, but she didn't. Instead, she was standing perfectly upright. It was DJ who was in peril. He was dangling high in the air, Bella clenching his pants with her teeth. Bella's ears had stretched out like small wings, and she was floating in the air.

Pup stood where DJ had stood and was making mocking rhymes of his own: "Bully-bully, zoom-zoom. Bully-bully, boom-boom."

Pup turned to Dyna with a question: "Drop-drop? Plop-plop?"

Before Dyna could answer "Yes," Benny cut in. "Pup! No! If Bella plops DJ on his head, he'll get badly hurt!" Up in the air, Bella was snarling and seemed perfectly willing to drop the bully. "Make him promise to stop bullying. Make him apologize. That'll be enough," Benny pleaded with Pup. "Don't hurt him. No plop-plop. No ouch-ouch. Just make him promise." DJ was crying and begging to be put back on solid ground.

Bella glided down to the ground. She appeared to have grown in size, as she was now standing eye-to-eye with DJ. Then Bella spoke! Her voice was soft, but it demanded honesty. "Do you promise?"

DJ was tongue-tied with fear, and he struggled to speak. "I'll st …sto …stop bullying. I …I …pro … prom …promise."

"Please apologize too," Bella prompted.

This time, DJ didn't stumble on his words and simply said, "I'm sorry, Dyna, Paco, and Benny."

Bella stared into DJ's eyes for several seconds, and simply said, "Go." Dismissed, DJ slipped and slid down the muddy hill, and quickly headed home. Bella's growling and snarling had made all the other kids flee in fear. Standing atop the hill, only Dyna and Paco remained. Dyna wasn't the least bit bothered by the whole incident. Paco, on the other hand, stood in disbelief. Stunned, he kept muttering over and over, "Pup can talk. Bella can fly. Bella can talk …"

Paco kept repeating out loud what echoed in Benny's head. Bella can talk! Bella can talk! Benny wondered, did she talk only when absolutely necessary?

CHAPTER 4

The Color
of Stars

It didn't matter that Bella was tired, or that Paco was in a bit of shock. Pup was invigorated by all the excitement and wanted to play. One of his ears wiggled about, pointing to the saucers scattered on the ground. The other ear held steady, pointing toward Mount Alta Vista. The valley town of Prickly Pear was surrounded on three sides by mountain ranges. Snow-capped Alta Vista was the highest mountain in the northern range.

"Slip-slip, slide-slide. Zip-zip. Glide-glide," Pup kept repeating.

Pup's enthusiasm gave Bella new energy. She flapped her ears in an upbeat "da-da-dah da-di-dah" cadence, most certainly a "yes." They were going to the mountain!

With a quizzical look, Benny inquired, "And how the heck are we supposed to get up there?"

Just how they'd get to Alta Vista became obvious when Bella's already long body stretched out even more and her already floppy ears grew even floppier.

All her folds of skin began to disappear, the longer she grew. She looked like a colorful hot-air balloon being inflated for flight.

As Bella grew bigger, Pup pressed the infinity symbol on his orange belly patch. The "infinity pocket" opened into a pouch. Pup stuck his snout in and pulled out a miniature assortment of snow suits, rubber boots, gloves, and ski caps. Almost immediately, the gear expanded to full size.

Benny looked for Paco's reaction. Paco gave him one. "I guess the infinity sign really does mean Pup's pouch holds everything."

Benny was very familiar with Paco's sense of humor. Paco liked to joke by acting like something wasn't much of a big deal when it really was. But now, Benny could tell Paco was not joking. Paco was as confused as Benny about what they had just witnessed.

Cautiously, Benny poked his finger into one of the gloves. It was real, not some kind of virtual projection.

Paco was not as pokey. He was already slipping into his snowsuit.

Dyna stood still, speechless, until she spoke. "Blue's boring. Do you have a pink snowsuit?" All three snowsuits were the same color, navy blue.

She promptly added, "Do you have a pink cap too?" The boots, gloves, and caps were all black.

Pup dug back into his pouch, only to emerge empty-handed.

"Not-Not. Got-got," he said with disappointment.

"I take back what I said before," Paco remarked. "Pup's pouch doesn't hold everything."

Pup was first to hop on Bella's back, followed by Benny and Paco.

Before joining them, Dyna asked if Pup had sleds in his pouch. Outfitted in boring blue, Dyna had learned the limitations of Pup's pouch the hard way.

Without even looking, Pup knew the answer. His ears drooped down, and he shook his head "no."

Dyna ran down the hill and borrowed three snow saucers, abandoned by the kids who had fled the scene. When Dyna returned, Bella extended her front right leg for Dyna to use as a step. As Dyna stepped up, Bella gave her an approving wink, as if to say, "Way to think ahead!"

All aboard, Pup pulled tinted ski goggles out of his pouch. Once the goggles were full size, he passed them out.

Benny and Paco each got goggles with black frames and black straps. Dyna's were different.

"Yay! Pup's got pink goggles!" she cheered. Even the strap was a bright pink. Dyna's faith in Pup's pouch was restored.

Next, Pup pulled out odd-looking goggles with thick frames and bulging lenses for himself. The lenses made it look as if Pup's eyes were going to pop out of his head.

"Don't those coke-bottle lenses make you dizzy?" Benny asked.

Paco had a different question. "Can I try them on?"

Pup answered Paco, "Say-say, nay-nay. Goggle-goggle, doggle-doggle."

"What are 'doggles?'" Paco asked.

"Doggles are just for dogs," Bella responded. "They'll make a person dizzy." Bella went on to explain. "Doggles are one of Pup's inventions. Dogs can't see red and green, but, with doggles, they can."

Bella was last to get her eyewear, a stylish pair of aviator sunglasses, the kind fighter-jet pilots wear. Benny held back asking if Pup had an extra pair, not wanting to trouble Pup over fashion. With everyone goggled up, all was now "go" for take-off.

As Bella's ears stretched even wider, the whole crew slowly lifted off the ground. Bella floated up over the foothills, letting a breeze carry her into Creek Canyon where she caught an updraft, and headed toward Alta Vista.

The mountaintop couldn't be more different from the desert valley below. It was covered with a pine tree forest so thick there was no place to land. Bella let the windstream carry her over the highest peak to the other side of the mountain, where Benny spotted the Mount Alta Vista Space Observatory. The observatory was situated high in the mountain to give a clearer view of the stars. The slope around the observatory was cleared of trees and was a perfect place to set down.

As soon as Bella touched down, Pup couldn't contain his excitement. He was not excited by the mountain of snow, but by the observatory's dome. Dancing, Pup made a foot-kicking leap and proclaimed, "Dome -dome. Home-home."

Bella's back proved to be an unreliable dance floor. Upon landing, Pup lost his footing and tumbled off and sank deep into the snow. Laughing, Paco hoisted

Pup up by the hourglass spot on his neck, just as Benny had done the night before when Pup tried to make his great escape from the bathtub.

"What's gotcha so excited, mi pupito?" Paco asked.

Pup shook off the snow, lifted his front paw, flapped his ears and repeated, "Dome-dome. Home-home."

Benny assumed Pup mistook the dome for someone's home and explained, "You're right, Pup. That is a dome, but no one lives in it. It's not a house. There's a telescope inside."

Benny knew a great deal about the telescope because every year Benny's science teacher, Ms. Clark, took her class on a field trip to the Alta Vista Observatory. Benny's class had recently made the bus trip up the narrow, winding mountain road.

Benny wanted to teach Pup about the telescope, but was unsure how best to accomplish that. Pup was a challenging student—his vocabulary was limited, but his comprehension seemed limitless.

Benny recalled what he'd learned from the astronomer during the class tour. "The telescope under the dome uses color to measure how hot stars are. Blue stars are the hottest and red stars are the coolest. Yellow stars, like our sun, are in between."

Paco had been on the same field trip. He added, in his own words, "There are also white stars. White stars are made up of so many colors that it fools our eyes into seeing only white."

Dyna didn't want to be left out. "Snow is white, so it's made of all the colors too."

Lifting his goggles, Benny squinted at the snow glaring back at him. He knew Dyna had said the first thing that popped into her head, but he wondered if, perhaps, she might be right.

As Benny lowered his goggles, Paco asked, "Do you think Pup understood us?"

Benny replied, "I don't know. But let's not make him take a test. I hate tests."

"Me too," Paco agreed.

Pup was quick to point out, "Play-play, day-day."

Pup was right. It was Sunday, a day off from school. It was a day to play!

CHAPTER 5

Runaway Train

The road that wound and sloped up to the observatory was perfect for sledding, except for one problem. There was too much snow! The saucers sank in so deeply that it was impossible to get any forward momentum. Bella had a remedy. She used her curved sword tail, wagging it back and forth, to cut a path. It took her only three minutes to clear a quarter-mile run.

Almost as much fun as Bella's run was the ramp Pup built at its end. Paco called the ramp "Pup's Revenge," since the saucer rider was launched high into the air and buried deep in a snowbank upon landing. The frosty burial was not unlike Pup's slip-jig tumble into the snow. Bella dug the kids out after each run and flew them back up to the start.

Pup stayed at the bottom, working to add more snow to his ramp. Pup's ramp grew more formidable with each run.

Yesterday, Benny had shaped the snow into a snowman. Today, he had a different idea.

"You two keep sliding. I'm gonna stay here and make a tunnel for Pup's ramp." Benny loved building things and snow was a wonderful building material.

Before flying Paco and Dyna back to the starting place, Bella used her tail to pile snow along the bottom of the run to help Benny get started.

Benny got busy. For him, designing and building was fun, not work at all. When he grew up, Benny wanted to build things, although he couldn't say exactly what. How could he say what if he hadn't invented them yet?

Each time Paco and Dyna zoomed past, Benny stepped back to assess progress. With Pup's help, he was adding about a foot each minute.

Benny proposed, "Hey Pup, what if we work for fifty minutes and make the tunnel fifty feet long?"

Pup approved. "Fifty-fifty, nifty-nifty."

After a few more runs, Paco lost interest in sliding, and joined Benny and Pup on the tunnel construction project. Dyna slid two more times, which wasn't as much fun anymore. She joined the tunnel-building.

All working together, the rate of progress doubled. After fifty minutes, Benny declared the project complete. The snow tunnel was one hundred feet long!

The tunnel gave Paco an idea. "Let's link together and go through the tunnel like a train."

Benny advised caution. "We may go into the tunnel like a train, but we'll shoot off the ramp like a rocket."

Benny's warning only sold Pup on Paco's idea. "Soar-soar! Roar-roar!"

Clapping her gloves together, Dyna cheered, "I wanna be a rocket too!"

Bella assembled the team at the top of the run, a desert sliding squad as inexperienced as even the one from Jamaica. Taking the lead, Dyna sat down first on her saucer, with Pup on her lap. Paco was second, locking his legs across Dyna's waist. Benny was next, his legs around Paco. Bella stood upright, the "pusher" behind her crew.

Just as Benny settled into position, Pup's "doggled" eyes rose like two full moons over the back of Dyna's shoulders. "Need-need, speed-speed."

Benny was trying to figure out what Pup meant. Then, Pup distributed helmets—four black ones and one pink one.

When all were helmeted, Benny felt Bella's two big paws clasp his shoulders. The "push" began. Benny could hear Bella's claws clicking into the ice for traction, just like his baseball cleats clicked on the kitchen floor. Benny even heard Mom's shout in his head.

"Take those cleats off right now, young man!"

Bella's high-thrust push matched that of even the gold medal Olympic team. They started out fast and only got faster. Their combined weight and the packed-down track added to their velocity.

Halfway down the run, they had already reached breakneck speed.

Like a runaway train, the sliders flew into the tunnel. Everything turned bright white—every color blurred together! Benny counted, "One thousand one, one thousand two, one thous—"

The train shot out the tunnel like a cannonball.

Paco must have had the exact same impression, as he shrieked like a banshee, "CANNONBAAAAL!!!"

Midway to wherever they were headed, the "Cannonball Express" began to wobble and shake. The front zigged left and the back zagged right. The train twisted, then jackknifed. The front saucer spun loose, Pup still aboard. Dyna was not. The other saucers stayed attached, only flipped upside down.

Benny saw Dyna suspended helplessly in mid-air as Pup and the saucer headed up and away. He grabbed her arm, and with all his might, pulled her aboard the engineless, tumbling train, all the time watching Pup spin off into the distance.

Luckily, the train was bound for a deep snow embankment one hundred feet beyond any previous jump. Their impact was about the same as dropping into a cushy pillow, except a pillow would be much warmer.

Bella extracted everyone from the snow and deposited them next to "Pup's Revenge." Without saying a word, she headed off in the direction Pup had flown.

Paco was not his usual joking self. He was worried. "I hope Pup's okay. Last I saw, he was flying up over the trees. This mountain's 9,157 feet tall. That's a long way down."

Dyna was less concerned. "Good thing he's got his helmet on."

Benny was worried too, until he wasn't. His mind had a way of ridding itself of worry by converting it into a math problem. Focusing on math made him feel calmer. He could catch details that he otherwise might miss in a panic. His world would move in slow motion.

It was this skill that always earned him the first base position on the baseball team. He never missed making a catch, even those throws that bounced in the dirt. It's why DJ attacked him from behind. Head on, Benny would have easily dodged the snowball. DJ would've looked foolish.

Now Benny found himself wondering—just how fast was the Cannonball Express going when it shot out of the tunnel?

He started to solve the problem: *If we went 100 feet in 2 seconds, then, since there's 60 seconds in a minute, we would go 60 times 50 feet in 1 minute. That's 3000 feet per minute. Since there's 60 minutes in an hour...*

Benny saw the flash out of the corner of his eye, not too high, just to the right of the sun, which was low in the western sky. It was a reflection. Perhaps off an airplane, Benny first thought. There was a second flash. The object was getting closer. Benny had a new thought, wasn't Dyna's saucer silver?

There was yet another flash. This was different. It held an array of colors. Benny let the others know.

"Look. Up over there. Just above and to the right of the sun. Bella's coming back."

"Where?" Paco asked. "I don't see a thing."

"There"—Benny pointed—"shade the sun with your hand."

"I see. I see," Dyna rejoiced. "And she's got Pup and the saucer."

"I see them now too." Paco said. "How did you see them from so far away?"

Teasing Paco, Benny replied, "Pup trusted me with a special pair of goggles. They give me superpower vision!"

Bella landed and Pup hopped down, not showing the slightest hint of trepidation over what must have been a harrowing, death-defying ride. All Pup did was open his pouch and pull out a jar of peanut butter, a jar of prickly pear jelly, and a loaf of bread. It was as if Pup had just returned from a quick run to the grocery store.

Before anyone could say anything, Dyna declared, "Look. Pup got me lunch!"

Paco had a different take. "I think the food's for all of us."

His pouch still open, Pup passed Benny a spreading knife.

As Benny took the knife, Paco teased Benny back. "Now, Pup's trusting you with a 'super powerful' spreading knife." Paco's sense of humor was back.

Benny's newly assigned task came with one major drawback. As fast as he could make sandwiches, the others gobbled them down. Benny finally got one to eat himself. There were only three slices of bread left, two of which were the heels. He made a double-decker sandwich for himself, peanut butter on the top deck and prickly pear jelly on the bottom.

Bella turned down a sandwich, perfectly content just to lick out the jars.

To top off lunch, Pup pulled out cups, along with a thermos of steaming hot chocolate. His ears had three jumbo marshmallows skewered on them. The treat gave the kids energy to climb on Bella's back for the ride home.

CHAPTER 6

Nicknames

The sun was setting over the western mountain range as the group glided back down to the valley. Their descent quickened the pace of the sunset, and soon the sky was lit with colors. Seeing a sunset while floating in the sky made it even more spectacular. Somewhere on the other side of the world, the sun was rising. That sunrise, Benny thought, couldn't possibly match the beauty of a desert sunset.

Bella touched down behind Paco's house. She was careful not to let a grown-up see her fly, so she landed on the outside of the adobe brick wall that surrounded the backyard. Bella was returning to her normal size. Her skin folds reappeared and her ears returned to their usual floppiness.

After removing his snow gear, Benny realized he hadn't noticed how Pup had packed up the knife, thermos, and cups in his pouch, just before leaving the mountain. Benny figured re-pouching was the reverse of un-pouching, and wanted to watch the rest of the gear shrink down in size. The process wasn't what Benny expected. Pup simply touched an item with his paw and it vanished.

While all the activity behind the house didn't catch the eye of any adult, the commotion didn't escape Guapo's ears.

From inside the house, Guapo started barking excitedly, "Woof-woof! Guau-guau! Woof-woof! Guau-guau!"

"I'd better get Guapo before he gets too loud," Paco said to Bella and Pup. "He'd want to meet both of you, anyway."

Paco hurried to get his dog.

As Paco closed the backyard gate behind himself, Benny asked Bella, "Can you tell what Guapo's saying?"

Laughing, Bella responded, "He's saying 'I know you're there. Come get me!'"

Benny was embarrassed he'd even asked the question.

Dyna had been listening, and she had a different question, "Does Guapo talk in English or Spanish?"

This time Bella gave a serious answer. "He talks in both. Like Paco, Guapo's bilingual."

"I don't understand. How can a dog talk in two languages?" Benny asked.

"If you listen closely, you can hear Guapo barking the sounds 'woof-woof' and 'guau-guau.' 'Woof-woof' is English and 'guau-guau' is Spanish. Throughout the world, dogs bark a bit differently, depending on the language of their people."

Benny was listening closely to Guapo's bark when it stopped. Paco had set him free.

Dyna broke the silence with a question. "What do dogs in France say?" French poodles were Dyna's favorite kind of dog.

"Ask Pup," Bella advised. "He's an expert in double-bark canine languages."

"Well, Pup, what do dogs in France say?" Dyna asked.

Pup responded quickly, "Vaf-vaf! Vaf-vaf!"

"What do dogs in China say?" Dyna asked, but Pup didn't answer because, just then, Paco returned with Guapo.

Guapo was a handsome dog. In fact, his very name meant "handsome" in Spanish. His snout was long and proud. He had a broad chest that tapered to a thin waist. His chocolate fur shined, as if it had been buffed.

Bella acknowledged Guapo with a rather quiet "Woof-woof. Guau-guau."

Benny thought Bella's fur took on a tinge of red. He wondered, can dogs blush?

Bella turned her attention from Guapo to Paco. "Instead of saying goodbye, Francisco, I'll say hasta luego."

Paco was confused, not because Bella spoke Spanish, but because she knew his formal name. "How'd you know my real name? Only my mom and dad ever call me Francisco."

Bella answered, "I know much about your namesake. The nickname Paco honors Saint Francis of Assisi, who's renowned for his love of animals. The nickname means 'Compassionate One,' so it suits you well."

Hearing Bella explain Paco's nickname made Dyna curious, "What's a saint? My nickname is Dyna. Am I named after a saint, like Paco?"

Dyna asked the questions to anyone in the group who might answer, and Paco answered her first. "Saints are good people who set good examples. You can only be one after you die."

Benny knew how Dyna got her nickname and answered, "Dyna, you're not named after a saint. Your full name is Theresa Nicole Tratten, so your initials are TNT. TNT is the same thing as dynamite. Dynamite explodes easily."

Dyna pondered the two answers for a few seconds, then proclaimed, "I don't think DJ will ever become a saint!"

Bella laughed again. "People can change, Dyna."

Benny looked west to see the sun descending behind the mountains. In a few more minutes, it would be gone, leaving only its rays.

Benny turned to Bella. "We've got to go now. We're supposed to be home before sunset."

Pup jumped up on Bella's back. Pup hadn't re-pouched the goggles Paco had worn on Alta Vista.

"Take-take. Sake-sake." Pup wanted Paco to keep the goggles for memory's sake.

Paco accepted the gift. He tried to say "thank you," first in English, then in Spanish, but no words came out. His voice faltered. Instead, Paco gave Bella and Pup a goodbye hug.

Again, Paco unlatched the back gate, pulled it open, and entered the backyard. This time, he was side-by-side with Guapo. The gate swung closed, the latch clicking tightly behind them.

The sun had now completely fallen behind the mountains. Benny and Dyna were going to be getting home late.

CHAPTER 7

The Wolf of Trattino

When Benny and Dyna got back to their house, Mom was standing by the front door, waiting. She wasn't smiling.

"You're late. Where've you been?" Mom was mad.

Dyna answered truthfully, "Bella flew us up to the mountaintop to play in the snow!"

Mom dismissed this answer as typical Dyna make-believe talk. Her attention now focused entirely on Benny.

"DJ's mom called. She said that the 'rainbow dog' viciously attacked DJ. She said DJ is traumatized. She's going to call the police. I asked her to hold off until you got home, so I could get your side of the story."

Benny gave his side of the story. As he described DJ's insults against Paco, Mom's face turned red and blood vessels bulged on her forehead, the same as Paco's reaction to DJ's bullying.

When Benny told how DJ grabbed Dyna by the hair and threw her down, Mom finally spoke, "I should've dealt with this yesterday, when DJ hit you in the face with that snowball. Boys will be boys, I thought. I was wrong. DJ's out of line."

Mom got down on one knee, wrapped her arms around Bella's neck, and said two words, "Thank you."

Mom told Benny and Dyna to join Dad at the dinner table, and she quickly headed into the den and shut the door.

Sunday was always a family "takeout" day, and there were two large pizza boxes stacked on the table, still steaming. They couldn't have been there too long. Printed on the box lid was "Gubbino's—Pizza Molto Delizioso." Benny's stomach growled with hunger. Gubbino's was his favorite.

As he sat at the table, snarfing down his first slice, Benny could hear fragments of Mom's call back to DJ's mom. "…bloody lip yesterday … yanking a child down by her hair …"

Mom's voice grew louder, and Benny heard full sentences.

"Where does a kid even learn such hate language? What DJ called Paco was horrible. I'm the one who should be calling the police."

Dad could tell Benny was intently listening in on what was fast becoming an adult conversation, so Dad devised a diversion.

"Did you know Paco is the nickname for Saint Francis of Assisi, the patron saint of animals?"

"We know. Bella already told us," Dyna answered.

Dad chuckled, "Well, did Bella tell you the most famous story, the one about Saint Francis and the hungry wolf?"

Dad's ploy worked. Benny and Dyna were not familiar with the story, and both wanted to hear it. Under the table, Bella's and Pup's ears perked up too. All were distracted from Mom's conversation.

Dad hesitated before starting, glancing around the room, then proceeded. "Just outside the small Italian village of Gubbino, there lived a big, bad wolf who terrorized the villagers. The wolf even snatched up small children who were out playing too late. ..."

Benny rolled his eyes. Normally, Benny tolerated Dad's awkward storytelling, but Dad was off to a really shaky start. Benny expressed his literary concerns.

"This story is lame. You just copied the village name from the pizza box. And you're stealing 'big, bad wolf' from 'Little Red Riding Hood.' And you're completely making up the part about snatching kids who come home late."

Dad defended himself. "I don't have a photographic memory. You can't expect me to know every small village in Italy. If it helps, I'll change the village name from Gubbino to Trattino, and the villagers are called 'Trattens.'"

Dyna was thrilled with this change. "The villagers have the same name as us!"

Dad had won Dyna over to his side. Benny had no choice but to accept the revision, as Dad continued with the tale.

"Saint Paco was quietly leading his burro, Benito, through the tiny village of Trattino. It was early in the morning, and he didn't want to wake the villagers. Saint Paco was halfway down the village's one dirt road when Benito sat down and started braying loudly. The burro was stubborn and brayed louder as Saint Paco tugged on him.

"It wasn't long before the Trattens all woke up and poured out onto the road to see what the racket was. Good thing too, because, of course, the Trattens recognized Paco and begged him to fix a great misfortune that had befallen Trattino. A molto grande wolf was snatching village elders who stayed out too late drinking at the local pub."

Dad paused, repeating "molto grande wolf" twice with an exaggerated Italian accent.

Dad gave two thumbs up in appreciation of Benny's earlier literary criticism.

"Thanks. 'Molto grande wolf' is much better than 'Big Bad Wolf.' It gives the tale a more authentic Italian flavor. Plus, I avoid copyright hassles with Little Red Riding Hood, Incorporated."

Dad picked up where he left off.

"Saint Paco agreed to help and headed into the woods without a weapon of any sort to befriend the molto grande wolf. The wolf spotted Saint Paco and was charging at him when Paco calmly said, 'Ya gotta try this.' The wolf skidded to a stop, and his nostrils flared into the air where Paco was dangling a big slice of pizza. It was Gubbino's famous thin crust—"

Stopping mid-sentence, Dad corrected himself. "Excuse me. I said Gubbino's, but I meant Trattino's. Of course, Gubbino's didn't exist back then. … It was Trattino's famous thin crust, double cheese, pepperoni pizza."

At this point, Mom returned to the dining room and sat down at the table.

"Don't let me interrupt," is all she said. Not a word about her phone call.

Dad returned to the story.

"Still holding the pizza, Saint Paco asked the wolf nicely, 'Tell me why you ate the village elders?'"

"The wolf explained, 'I'm hungry and must eat to stay alive.'"

"Saint Paco replied, 'Try this. If you think it tastes better than the villagers, I think we can strike a bargain.'"

"The wolf wolfed down the pizza and loved it. 'Wow! That's delicious. Way tastier than gray-bearded, sour men. And there's no end to the topping combinations. Let's make a deal!'"

"Paco returned to Trattino with the wolf at his side and brokered an accord. If the Trattens agreed to give the wolf pizza every day, the wolf agreed not to eat any of the townspeople. The oldest village elder, Dynella, shook the wolf's paw to seal the deal. Dynella had lived to the ripe old age of thirty-two because she didn't frequent the village pub. And so, the molto grande wolf and the Trattens lived happily together for 25 years, until the wolf died of old age."

Dad finished by asking if they knew the moral of the story.

Getting no takers, Dad finally revealed his answer.

"The moral is people can change. Even DJ deserves a chance to change."

Glowering, Mom expressed a different opinion. "Some people will never change. Cruelty is in their nature. When dealing with a bully like DJ, you have to fight fire with fire."

Dad replied, "It's also possible to fight fire with a bucket of water. DJ is still young."

Dyna gave her two cents' worth. "Bella didn't plop DJ on his head like me and Pup wanted. She gave him a second chance 'cause Benny asked her to."

"Perhaps Bella was right," Mom said, her glower fading. "Maybe the moral of the wolf story isn't that people can change, but that they deserve a chance to change."

No one saw, but under the table Bella wagged her tail.

Mom surveyed the table. Usually two large-size pizzas made for leftovers for Monday's lunch. There was only one slice left.

"Dyna," Mom asked, "just how much pizza did you feed the dogs?"

Dyna didn't answer because she'd fallen asleep, upright in her chair. Dad carried her up to bed, and Pup followed up after them.

Benny had trouble falling asleep, worried the police would show up any moment to arrest Bella. Mom hadn't said anything about her talk with DJ's mom. Whatever the outcome, Bella was not losing sleep over it. She was snoring away, unconcerned. As Benny petted the sleeping dog, his own worry drifted away. How in the world could the police ever apprehend a suspect who can escape simply by flying out a window? Even if they caught her, Pup would have a hacksaw to cut her free of the cuffs!

As the attacking wolf closed in, Saint Francis cried out: "Come hither, brother wolf; I command thee, in God's name, neither to harm me nor anybody else."

Marvelous to tell, no sooner had Saint Francis made the sign of the cross, than the terrible wolf, closing his jaws, stopped running, and coming up to Saint Francis, lay down at his feet as meekly as a lamb.

– From the tale of St. Francis of Assisi and the Wolf of Gubbio, dated 1220

CHAPTER 8

Flight into Night

Benny didn't remember falling asleep, but it was well past midnight when he was awakened by Pup licking his face.

"Bella-Bella, Pup-Pup, varoom-varoom, zoom -zoom."

Benny knew what this meant. Bella and Pup were getting ready to return home, wherever that might be. Benny's best guess was that Bella and Pup did, indeed, live among the stars. Benny even suspected that being away from the stars drained Bella's strength. She needed to return home to regain her energy, like a battery that needed to be recharged.

Benny was glad Pup woke him so they could say goodbye.

"Thanks for coming here. I'll miss you both. We'll all miss you, even Dad, though he wouldn't ever tell you so."

Instead of the "Bye-Bye" Benny expected, Pup replied, "You-you, too-too. Varoom-varoom. Zoom-zoom."

Benny could not tell if Pup was asking or telling, but Pup was clearly talking about a chance to go with them.

Benny felt his heart pounding, like never before. "Is that even possible?"

Bella walked over and rubbed her chin against Benny's leg.

"Yes, it's possible. Pup has the power to grant travel to the Star Realm, although he rarely extends such an offer."

Benny was overjoyed at the prospect of seeing Pup's and Bella's world. A giant hug to Bella and a kiss on Pup's cheek served as Benny's "Yes."

Bella spoke in her softest voice yet. "The Star Realm will be full of surprises. I must spoil one surprise before we leave. Max is there. Max may be gone from this world, but not from ours. I tell you this ahead of time, because you must understand—Max can't come back home with you. That's not possible."

Benny often dreamed of Max, but, outside of a dream, he never imagined he'd get to see Max again.

"I promise I won't complain. I'll be thankful if I can see Max for only a minute."

Bella perked up, amused. "I think we can arrange for more than just a minute."

While Benny was talking with Bella, Pup laid out a baggy spacesuit on Benny's bed. Next to the space suit was a helmet with a dark visor.

After Benny zipped himself into the spacesuit and attached the helmet, Pup gave Benny a pamphlet with flight instructions:

1. Please keep your spacesuit on at all times, as we must cross the vacuum of space to reach our destination.

When we arrive, you'll no longer need the suit, as there is air and gravity similar to Earth.

2. Your suit is airtight, and your helmet must be properly sealed to it at all times.

3. If you suspect an air leak, tap Pup on the shoulder twice. Pup has an emergency oxygen tank in his pouch. He will connect the oxygen and find and repair the leak.

Benny read the instructions closely, even though they were a lot like those given on an airplane where most passengers paid no attention.

After double-checking Benny's helmet, Pup placed aviator glasses on Bella. They were the same ones she'd worn on the flight to Mount Alta Vista, only now the glasses had a fitted earpiece that was attached by wire to a microphone in front of Bella's mouth. She looked more like a pop star ready to take the stage than an astronaut. Last, Pup put on the kaleidoscope doggles.

Benny had always thought "space" was the wrong name for space. "Space" was an empty void. Now, as he climbed on Bella's back with Pup, he knew he was right. Where he was venturing was anything but space! It was a realm of unimagined worlds.

Bella slowly exited the window and navigated the space between the house and the palo verde tree in the front yard.

The Earth quickly disappeared behind the trio. Bella was speeding directly toward the bright star Pup had pointed to from Benny's bedroom window the night before. As the bright star grew closer and closer, Benny's spacesuit grew warmer. His suit was bordering on hot, when Bella's voice came over a speaker inside his helmet. "The large white helium star we're approaching is my home star. Its nickname is the 'Dog Star.'"

Bella added with pride, "It's the brightest star in the night sky!"

Benny checked if the communications worked both ways. "Testing, testing. One, two, three. Testing, testing: Can you hear me?"

"Loud and clear," Bella replied.

"Well, I wanna let you know," Benny said, "it's getting pretty hot in this spacesuit."

Bella reassured Benny, "Don't worry. It will cool off soon."

Bella had no sooner said that, when a much smaller blue star began to orbit in front of the bright-white larger star. The smaller star began to change color from blue to red. It was absorbing heat energy from the bigger star. Benny's spacesuit started to cool off.

Bella's voice again came in over his helmet's speaker. "The small star moving in front of the Dog Star is Pup's home star. Pup's star orbits mine. When Pup's star comes into exact alignment with the center of the Dog Star, a portal will open, and we'll fly through it."

Judging by its rate of movement, it was going to be a minute before Pup's star orbited to the center of the Dog Star. Benny used that minute for a question. "Does Pup's home star have a name?"

"It's nameless on Earth, but in the Star Realm, Pup's home is known as the 'Miracle Star.' It's a pure hydrogen star. The only known one of its kind in the universe."

As the Miracle Star moved closer to the center of the Dog Star, Bella advised, "There will be stellar wind turbulence as we travel through the portal. Please hold on securely to Pup to ensure safe transit."

"How bad is the turbulence going to be?" Benny asked, his voice reverberating in his helmet.

"Somewhere between a moon bounce and being shot out of a cannon," Bella replied. Benny had already been shot out of a cannon once that day, so the moon bounce was his preference.

The Miracle Star presented itself as a bullseye, and Bella sped into it.

All aboard were blasted by a heavy wind and the wild ride began. Benny teetered up, tottered down, and then bounced all around. Twice in one day, Benny thought. Benny and Pup clung to each other, not because they were frightened, but for safety. They emerged in the Star Realm.

Once through, the flight became perfectly calm.

Pup exclaimed, "Near-near! Here-here!" Even though Pup didn't have a microphone attached to his doggles, Benny could hear him clear as day—Pup was that excited!

"VAROOM!"

Ten, nine, eight,
Space awaits...
Seven, six, five,
No time for goodbyes...
Four, three, two...
A doggled-dog crew!
One...
BLAST OFF!!!

– by Benny

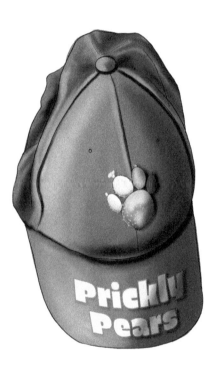

CHAPTER 9

The World Beyond

Bella made a gentle descent toward an emerald green island that floated off in the distance. It was shaped like a four-leaf clover—the rare, lucky kind of shamrock. At the island's center was a yellow, flashing beacon. Bella was tracking the bright flashes, as if she were approaching an airport runway. Benny assumed the beacon was their destination.

As Bella glided closer, Benny could see that the beacon was a gleaming gold dome. The dome was the centerpiece of a tremendous white-marble palace that stood alone in the middle of a vast field. When Bella reached the dome, she banked to the right and made a gentle descent over a reflecting pool that ran from the palace's entryway to an elegant gazebo. As Bella neared, the gazebo's octangular roof folded open and she made a perfect four-paw landing inside. As the roof folded closed, Bella announced, "We've reached our destination. There's air, gravity, and plenty of light, so you may remove your spacesuit and move about freely."

After taking off his helmet, zipping off his flight suit and handing them to Pup to re-pouch, Benny walked up to the gazebo's railing to gaze at the palace and its reflection in the water. The palace reminded Benny of a grand and glorious building called the Taj Mahal. The Taj Mahal made an impression on Benny because it was called one of the new Seven Wonders of the World. Benny imagined that the wonder right in front of him could pick the Taj Mahal up like a small baby.

As silly as it seemed, Benny also now wondered if Dyna might've been right about Bella being a queen.

Benny felt childish, but nevertheless asked, "Are you a queen? Is this your palace?"

Bella paused, thinking, before answering. "Dogs here call me 'Guardian.' It's an honored position, but a humble one. Instead of ruling, I serve. So, I suppose I'm the opposite of a king or queen."

Bella continued. "And this isn't my palace. It's the Observatory. It's the center of the Star Realm. Dogs come here to check on their people back on Earth."

Looking at the Observatory's golden dome reflecting in the water, Benny now understood Pup's happy dance when Bella set down atop snowy Alta Vista.

"Does the Observatory dome have a telescope in it like Alta Vista?" Benny asked.

"It has a telescope," Bella responded, "but the telescope isn't like the one at Alta Vista. It's different. I'll take you inside to see it shortly."

Bella next lifted her head and gave out a slow, "Ahh-wooooo!"

"I'm letting my brother know I'm here," Bella said. "He's supposed to meet me, but he always runs a bit late."

Benny had been curious about Bella's family, but she hadn't been very talkative on Earth. Here, she was rejuvenated, so Benny asked the one question he was most curious about. "Are you Pup's mom?" He added tactfully, "He doesn't much look like you."

Bella replied, "I'm not Pup's mom. Pup is a Driftling. His home star wandered into my star's orbit over 150,000 years ago, when I was a young pup myself. Since then, I've grown older, while Pup has not aged a day. He's as young today as the day he became my companion."

Bella's last remark caused Benny concern, as Benny thought of Pup as being a child Dyna's age.

"If you keep getting older, and Pup stays young, who'll care for him when you're gone?" Benny asked.

"Don't worry about Pup. Driftlings can take care of themselves. Some believe them to be time travelers. Others think they're from a realm not yet known to science. Some even think they're magical. I believe, when I'm gone, Pup will do what he always does—what's best."

Benny started to give his opinion about Pup being magical, when he was interrupted by a deep-voiced, "Ahh-wooooo!"

A big black and tan dog came bounding out of the high grass toward the gazebo. The approaching dog had features like Bella, with big floppy ears and loose folds of skin. There were differences, though. This dog had much longer legs than Bella, but a much shorter body. When he ran, his ears didn't skim nearly as close to the ground as Bella's. Bella's brother had a bad limp, which caused his left ear to gyrate instead of flap.

Bella gave out another howl, and soon sister and brother were standing together under the gazebo bellowing out Ahh-woooos! The joyful howling soon gave way to a lively conversation. The two dogs spoke in a baritone "oom-pah-pah" language that Benny didn't understand. As Bella and her brother laughed and chatted easily, Benny could make out only a few words, "Alta Vista," "Francisco," "TNT," and "Molte Grande." Apparently, Bella was recounting tales of her Earth adventure. Bella pronounced "molte grande" with un exaggerated Italian accent, so there was no doubt "Wolf of Trattino" made the highlights.

"Forgive me for being rude," Bella spoke in English, so Benny knew she was talking to him. "I should've made introductions first. I haven't seen Rigel in a long while and got caught up in the excitement!"

Bella made a formal introduction. "Benny, please meet my brother, Rigel."

Benny was wondering if he should reach out and shake Rigel's paw, when Bella turned to her brother and spoke a short sentence in Rigel's language. This sentence started with Rigel's name and ended with Benny's, so Benny was sure Bella was concluding the introduction: "Rigel, please meet Benny."

Rigel sat down with a perfectly straight back, proudly holding his chin high. He extended his right paw to shake Benny's hand. It was the most dignified pose

Benny had ever seen anyone ever make, dog or human. Benny shook Rigel's paw.

After making the introduction, Bella resumed her conversation with Rigel. This time, Benny could only decipher one word, "Max." The conversation was brief, and when it ended, Rigel headed off, howling into the field from where he came.

"Rigel is off to find Max," Bella explained. "It shouldn't take too long. He's already putting out the call." Soon howls were spreading throughout the field, as dog after dog took up the cause of finding Max.

As Rigel disappeared into the tall grass, Benny asked about Bella's family. "How many brothers and sisters do you have?"

"My family here is unlike yours on Earth. I don't have a mom and dad, like you do. I consider the Dog Star my parent. It's part of me and I'm part of it."

Bella then asked Benny an odd question, "Have you ever struck the coals in an outdoor fire with a stick and watched the sparks rise into the night sky?"

Benny had done this many times.

"I asked that question because I want to make a comparison," Bella explained. "My star and Rigel's star rose together from the same strike. We're similar, but different. He's a bloodhound. I'm a basset hound. Still, I call him my brother, as he's my closest kin."

Benny wanted to ask Bella about Rigel's limp, but was unsure if that would be rude.

Instead, Benny posed a question he was less interested in.

"What's the language Rigel speaks?"

Bella's answer only made Benny more intrigued about Rigel's limp. "Rigel speaks the ancient language of the first bowhunter, a Man-Chieftain named Orion. Rigel's name itself is from the Chieftain's language and means 'Right Hand.' Rigel speaks only the Chieftain's language to honor his blood bond with Orion. This blood bond is why Rigel limps."

The excitement on Benny's face matched that of Pup's wildly wagging tail. It didn't matter that Pup had heard the "blood bond" story a thousand times before. His ears flared wide open in anticipation of hearing it again.

Benny spoke for them both. "Please, tell us the story!"

Bella began the tale.

CHAPTER 10

Rigel and the Bloodbond Arrow

"In the time before the written word," Bella started, "there was a terrible freeze. Ice crept over the Earth. This freeze was most cruel to the man-tribes, because man lived mostly by fishing. When the seas and rivers froze over, man lost his food source. Facing starvation, the tribes turned to hunting the wild animals of the forest for food. But they were unskilled hunters and had a distinctive fish odor that warned prey of their approach. Weaker animals easily avoided them and stronger predator animals easily tracked them. Man could not see at night and became an easy target for night-hunting panthers, onyx-toothed tigers, dire wolves, and sharp-taloned nighthawks. Even owls were lethal night predators, although the owls never preyed on people. Long-clawed bears and baboon-wolves were even so bold as to hunt man during the day."

Benny had never heard of baboon-wolves and was trying to imagine one. Bella read his thoughts. "You don't know about baboon-wolves because they're now extinct. Do you know what 'extinct' means, Benny?"

Benny knew. "It means that none are left and there won't ever be any more."

Bella wagged her tail as a show of approval, and then proceeded. "Baboon-wolves were despicable beasts, half wolf and half baboon. They mastered walking upright, freeing up their front legs to become incredibly strong arms. They hunted in packs, camouflaging themselves in trees and dropping down on their prey. Some of the most vicious baboon-wolves learned how to carry and throw spears. These baboon-wolves became known as 'goon-wolves,' although some called them 'hell-wolves' because their leader was named Hades. The goons hunted and captured every kind of animal, even weaker wolves. They held their captives for ransom and kept as slaves those who could not meet the high ransom."

Bella stopped herself. "I'm not sure I should continue. This story is more for grown-ups."

Benny urged on Bella, "I can take it. This story doesn't scare me at all. I know wild animals are dangerous. I know people can be dangerous and cruel and that owls aren't gentle pets. Owls catch rabbits."

Bella yielded to Benny's plea and continued. "During the great freeze, Rigel's clan of Snifferhounds faced starvation. Snifferhounds hunted by smelling out underground dens of smaller animals, like racoons, muskrats, and opossums. Because of the freeze, the Sniffers couldn't dig their prey out of the icy ground. Now, here's the worst part, Benny. They joined their cousins, the baboon-wolves and dire wolves, in hunting man. The Sniffers used their keen sense of smell and found hidden man-tribe encampments to be attacked. The Snifferhounds didn't take part in the carnage, but were always rewarded with a fair share of spoils for their help. The man-tribes were being wiped out."

Bella paused from her story to address Benny. "I can only regret the choice the Snifferhounds made. I can't change history, Benny. This history is a truth that mustn't be forgotten or denied. It's a history to learn from."

Bella then continued the story. "Man was near extinction. There was only one tribe left, which was led by Orion and his wife, Beatrix. This tribe survived not because it had the fiercest warriors, but because of Beatrix's genius and Orion's craftsmanship. Their camp was well-concealed because Beatrix had the idea to fashion fishing nets into camouflage netting. She invented domed ovens, called kilns, so the fire wouldn't reveal the camp's location. Orion discovered how to use the kilns to melt iron ore into digging trowels and spear tips. Beatrix figured out that odor gave away their location, so she brewed a masking scent from pine sap and sassafras roots. Orion used scent against the predators. He baited decoy camps with man-scent to lure bears, nightcats, wolves, and even baboon-wolves into ambushes.

"The last man-tribe survived five years without detection, but even great inventions and precautions were not enough to hide from Rigel's nose. Rigel had the keenest sense of smell of any animal to ever live. On one of the warmer summer days of the frozen years, a light wind stirred as the sun set in the west. On this sunset breeze, Rigel caught the faintest odor of a mankind newborn, its scent not yet masked with Beatrix's concoction.

"Rigel tracked the baby's scent when a green flash bolted across the sky. With that flash, the scent was gone. He had gotten a good fix on the scent and set off in that direction. Had he not stumbled right into Beatrix's camouflage netting, Rigel would've missed the hidden encampment altogether. But fate must always have its say.

"With a single howl, Rigel could have brought the wrath of his deadly cousins down on the last man-tribe, but Rigel made a different choice."

Benny couldn't contain his excitement, as he was sure he knew what happened next. "I betcha Rigel showed compassion to Orion, Beatrix, and the new baby. He became their friend and helped them survive. Rigel is just like Saint Francis!"

This last remark caused Bella to burst out laughing. "This time you're wrong, Benny! Rigel has many good qualities, but he's no saint! Rigel's a no-nonsense realist. His philosophy is 'Show your wagging tail and hide your sharp teeth.'"

As Bella had a habit of doing, she posed a question to Benny: "Do you recall how, just before our flight to Alta Vista, Dyna thought ahead about bringing saucers?" Of course, Benny remembered this, but he thought Bella's question was dumb: What do snow saucers have to do with sharp teeth and Rigel's choice?

Benny didn't say what he was thinking, but, again, Bella read his thoughts. "So, you think my question is a dumb one, right?"

It was pointless to try to fool Bella, so Benny admitted the truth, "Yes."

"Well, think about this," Bella spoke in her teaching voice. "Dyna thought ahead about a problem and took action to keep it from happening. Without her forethought, you would have had plenty of snow, but no sleds. Her forethought showed wisdom."

Benny now understood Bella's point. "Rigel made his choice not out of compassion, but because he was thinking ahead."

Before Bella could answer, Pup piped in, "Woosh-woosh, sting-sting." Benny had forgotten he was there. Pup sounded annoyed.

Bella gave Benny a smile. "Pup thinks you're interrupting the best part of the story. He wants you to keep quiet until I finish."

Benny remained quiet and Bella continued. "When Rigel arrived at the hidden camp, he marveled at the genius of the camouflage netting, fire kiln, and scent-masking balm. When he crept under the netting, Rigel observed one more ingenious invention that caused him to think ahead. Orion had taken the six-string musical harp Beatrix had created and fashioned it into a weapon. Rigel watched in amazement as Orion, a red-haired giant of a man, loaded a small spear, the earliest arrow, onto a harp string. As the giant drew back the arrow, his right hand brushed against his red beard, rattling the beads braided into it. When the rattling stopped, he released the arrow—a perfect bullseye."

Bella paused here, thinking to herself. She quietly spoke her thoughts. "What woman creates for beauty, man crafts for war." Benny knew he wasn't meant to overhear this, so he remained silent.

"Woosh-woosh, sting-sting." Pup was now impatient with Bella for not getting to the best part of the story.

"Okay, Pup," Bella reassured him. "No more interruptions."

"With this new invention, Rigel could foresee salvation for both mankind and dogkind. He was wise and knew what the future held. Once his cousin wolves had no more men to devour, the weaker hounds would become their next prey. Rigel was so certain of this that he took a great risk. Rigel gave out a low, soft howl, so only Orion could hear him. He anticipated that Orion would shoot an arrow at him, and Orion did. The arrow 'wooshed' faster through the air than Rigel could have ever imagined. Far too fast for Rigel to dodge. It stung him in the left shoulder. Instead of running or crying, Rigel sat up perfectly straight, with his chin held high. Proud and ready to die, Rigel extended his right paw to Orion.

"Orion recognized Rigel's gesture as one of friendship and respected the hound's courage. He accepted Rigel's paw and shook it, exactly as you shook it, Benny. Beatrix pulled out the arrow and nursed Rigel back to health. When he was healed, Rigel returned to his pack and convinced the Snifferhounds to ally with the last man-tribe. The Snifferhounds renamed their clan

Bloodhounds to honor the alliance sealed with Rigel's blood. Man and bloodhound kept each other warm on the most freezing nights. The hounds howled out warnings whenever they caught scent of an approaching threat. Man and bloodhound hunted together. All those of the man-tribe mastered shooting arrows, and soon the long-clawed bears, baboon-wolves, and dire wolves became the hunted."

Orion passed Benjamin to his wife, Beatrix, who quickly applied an herbal ointment to mask the baby's human scent.

- From this story's prologue, dated to a time unknown

CHAPTER 11

Reunion

As Bella finished her story, the howling that had rumbled into the distance echoed back toward where Benny was sitting with Bella and Pup in the gazebo. "They found Max!" Bella announced. "He's heading this way with his pack."

A dozen bellowing hound dogs were racing toward them. The lead dog was rusty red, with extremely long legs and wiry hair. There was no doubt this was Max. "Will he be able to talk like you and Rigel?" Benny asked.

"No. Max doesn't speak as Rigel and I do," Bella answered. "Here, Max is still your Max. Only those of us with a home star can speak human languages."

This pleased Benny immensely, as he loved Max just the way he was.

When the pack arrived, Max pounced on Benny, licking Benny's face as if it were an ice cream cone. Benny rubbed noses with his old pal, joyfully proclaiming the whole time, "Who'za best dog? Who'za best dog?"

Unable to restrain themselves any longer, the dogs in Max's pack joined in the celebration. Benny was covered in dog kisses.

Eventually, Bella gave out a sharp bark, as if to say, "That's enough. Let Max have time with his boy." The hounds broke up their celebration.

Sensing some envy, Benny kept his next hug short and refrained from saying, "Who'za best dog?"

Bella confirmed what Benny sensed. "Watching you with Max has made the hounds eager to see their own people back on Earth. We'll head to the Observatory with them, since I want to give you a tour."

Even though the hounds were eager to go, out of respect, they waited for Bella to lead the way. Accepting the honor, Bella led a happy parade down the steps of the gazebo and along the reflecting pool's walkway that ran right up to the Observatory. As they approached, Benny could see that the Observatory's entryway was not at ground level. This was because, as far as Benny could tell, the Observatory itself was not attached to the ground. It floated just one step above the surface. Benny took that one step up, with Max at his side.

The Observatory's entryway was a work of art, a truly majestic portico. Six gold pillars supported an arched roof decorated with elaborate etchings of …people. All kinds of people, doing simple things: Watching TV, eating a burger, playing ball. …The Observatory's towering doors had depictions too. The carvings were like those on the arch: People going about their daily lives. Nothing special, at least to people.

When Bella approached, the doors parted automatically. They didn't swing in or out, but slid back into the wall.

The inside of the Observatory wasn't at all what Benny was expecting. It was brightly lit, with water fountains and gardens spread throughout a gigantic open hall. Upon entry, every dog, except Max, put on a color-coded collar. Each collar had a small light bulb dangling from it. The collars came in five different colors, obviously corresponding to the size of the dogs' necks: yellow, XL; orange, L; red, M; green, S; and blue, XS.

Benny was curious and asked Bella, "What are the light bulbs for? There's plenty of light in here."

"The bulbs aren't for light," Bella answered. "They flash to let a dog know when a viewing helmet is available at Hercules' stand. That's where we're going now."

"Are the helmets for viewing people on Earth?" Benny asked.

"More than just viewing. It's almost like you're there," Bella answered.

Benny offered a comparison. "Kinda like a virtual reality headset?"

"Exactly like that," Bella said.

Benny scratched Max's head. "So, you've been watching over me this whole time, haven't you ole buddy?"

Max gave an affirmative tail wag.

Collars on, the hounds in Max's pack broke into smaller groups and headed off in different directions.

Bella explained, "All the dogs in Max's pack are from North America, so they've a bit of time on their paws before their people wake up. Hercules isn't about to give out viewing helmets just so dogs can watch their people sleep. Don't worry, though. There's plenty to do here. They won't be bored!"

One group put on bright orange vests. The vests were similar to life preservers kept on boats and planes. Strapped in, the dogs floated up into the air together, and then quickly flew off like a formation of geese.

"They're off to the play park," Bella said. "It's a bit of a distance away, so they've opted for the helium-filled jet vests. If you don't mind, I'd prefer to walk to Hercules. I've had enough flying for one day."

Benny didn't mind at all. While the jet vests looked like a bunch of fun, walking with Max by his side was so much better.

CHAPTER 12

"Quite the Celebrity"

With Pup perched on her back, Bella led Benny and Max onto a narrow trail that cut through a stand of woods. The trail was covered with pine needles mixed with red, orange, and gold leaves. It felt more like Halloween than wintertime. With a gust of wind, more leaves floated down. The gust carried a clear sound of "choo-choo." It was hard to tell where the sound had come from, as it was muffled by rustling leaves.

Benny weighed whether to ask Bella about the "choo-choo" or the wind. He was curious about both. He decided on the wind. "How can there be wind? We're inside a building?"

Bella countered with a question of her own. "How can there be trees? We're inside a building."

Benny knew what was behind Bella's response. He should look at the bigger picture for answers. Benny held back asking about the "choo-choo," now preferring to figure it out for himself.

The Halloween trail emerged from the woods and ended at an intersection with a cobblestone path. That path was perfectly straight and had a stone wall running next to it. Benny was just tall enough to peer over the wall. There were railroad tracks on the other side. Those tracks and the path ran parallel to each other, separated by the wall.

Bella was too short to see over the wall, but she knew what was there.

"The stone wall is a protective barrier from the tracks, so dogs don't wander in front of trains."

Bella took a right onto the cobblestone path. As Benny followed behind, he let his eyes wander down the tracks. Not too far ahead, he saw something peculiar. The rails ended at a giant merry-go-round! Benny refused to believe his eyes. He soon figured out his eyes were, indeed, mistaken. Instead of hobby horses bobbing up and down, there was a train engine rotating inside a railroad roundhouse!

Once aligned with the tracks on the other side of the wall, this train began moving toward them. The engine was pulling eight passenger cars, each filled with dogs barking wildly. Big heads jutted out of the first four cars, woofing. Smaller heads poked out of the last four cars, yapping. The train let out a whistle, "Choo. Choo."

"Dogs mostly come here by high-speed train," Bella said.

As the train passed, Benny noticed it didn't have wheels. It was floating.

A wheelless train, yet tracks. Benny just had to ask. "If the train doesn't have wheels, why are there tracks?"

Again, Bella echoed Benny's question back to him, "Why are there tracks?"

Always the teacher, Bella wanted Benny to answer his own question. Benny did. "The rails are magnetized to keep the train from floating away."

"A-plus," Bella responded, delighted with her student. "The train cars are metal and their walls contain pressurized helium, so they float. There's a precise balance between the rails' magnetism, their magnetic attraction to metal, and the pressurized helium."

After the train passed, Bella veered from the stonewall path and headed toward another, more normal sized, carousel that was near the roundhouse. A half-dozen dogs were standing on the carousel, their collar bulbs blinking. The dogs were gathered around a circular rack with helmets on it, sorted by size. The yellow XLs were on the top tier and blue XSs were on the bottom.

Instead of taking the ramp, Bella hopped onto the carousel, as Pup bounced around on her back like a buckeroo. Benny and Max stepped up without the slightest effort.

On the carousel, a burly bulldog was in a booth, pushing buttons and pulling levers to operate a mechanical claw. Benny watched the claw pick up a yellow XL off the rack and lower it gently onto the head of a mastiff. Helmet in place, the mastiff's collar stopped blinking.

"The booth operator is Hercules," Bella informed Benny. "He's in charge of railway operations at the Observatory." Hercules wore a red-striped railroad engineer's cap with the emblem of a winged train engine on the front of it. The engine had a big, round light on its front.

Hearing his name, Hercules looked up. When he spotted Bella, he gave out a proud "Oorah."

The other dogs all saw Bella too, and raced toward her. Benny stepped aside to avoid the onrush, but his sidestep was pointless. The dogs weren't rushing to see Bella, but to see him.

All the dogs frolicked at Benny's feet, vying for his attention. There was one exception though. The yellow-helmeted mastiff gave Benny a slobbery lick across the face.

Watching the love fest, Bella remarked, "My, oh my, aren't we quite the celebrity!"

Benny felt like an Olympic champion signing autographs for adoring fans. Max didn't mind sharing Benny one bit. Today, Max was one lucky dog who didn't need a viewing helmet because he had his boy with him!

Benny petted the dogs and scratched their heads as Bella conversed with Hercules. The two old friends spoke in a language that sounded harsh to Benny's ears. Among the guttural grunts and tricky tongue twisters, Benny could only make out a few words— "Benny," "Max," and "helmet." The rest sounded like Klingon.

"Hercules doesn't mind in the least if you examine one of the helmets," Bella said in English, so Benny knew she was addressing him.

Hercules pushed a button, pulled a lever, and the claw delivered an XL helmet right into Benny's hands. As Benny inspected the helmet, Hercules placed helmets on the heads of the dogs in Benny's fan club.

One helmet feature in particular intrigued Benny. There was a horseshoe magnet on the top, aimed skyward.

Benny paused before asking about the magnet, letting his brain spin on why it was there. Coming up with nothing, he finally asked, "What's the magnet for?"

Bella answered, "It's a plug. The horseshoe plugs into cables from the telescope. You'll see. That's where we're headed next."

Benny set the helmet down on the counter and thanked Hercules for allowing the hands-on inspection.

After Bella and Hercules spoke briefly, Bella said to Benny, "Hercules doesn't want you to leave without a souvenir. He wants you to stand still for just a second."

Benny stood still, as Hercules spun the claw around, lifted his red-striped engineer's cap off his own head, and placed it on Benny's.

Honored, Benny accepted the cap and again thanked Hercules.

A loud, high-pitched whistle blew. Benny looked over to see three old-fashioned wooden tram cars exit the roundhouse on a cable-car track. The lead car had a flat yellow roof, while the second car had an arched glass canopy that allowed much more headroom. The third car was a simple, flat-bed railcar with nothing on it, except an umbrella clothesline standing empty in its middle.

"That's the tram we'll be taking to the telescope," Bella explained.

The tram had wheels. Brimming with confidence from his recent "A-plus," Benny offered an explanation. "The tram has wheels because its cars are made of wood. The magnetized rails can't hold it down. It would float away."

"Impeccable reasoning," Bella lauded. "But wrong. Dogs are nostalgic. An old-fashioned tram ride brings happy memories of home."

Just then, Hercules pulled a cord and sounded a loud horn, as if he were the driver of a big-rig semi-truck. It was a signal to brace for motion, as the carousel was about to transport those aboard over to the tram.

"Since you're balanced on only two legs, you may want to grab a pole," Bella advised.

All around the carousel were vertical poles. They looked like the merry-go-round poles riders grip, only these poles didn't have riding horses attached to them. Benny grabbed the pole nearest to him.

The carousel gave a single jolt upwards and floated its passengers gently over to the tram. Benny didn't bother asking Bella how the carousel could float, certain he already knew the answer: Helium.

Hercules gave out a commanding bark. The helmeted dogs understood: "All aboard!" They trotted into the yellow-roofed car. Bella led Benny and Max over to the second car. She stepped aside as Benny and Max boarded first. Benny dipped his head, taking care not to bang it on the canopy. Once inside, he could stand up comfortably and look through the arched glass.

As she got on the tram, Bella remarked, straight-faced, "Hercules has added a special V.I.P. car for you. Celebrity status has its perks!"

Benny couldn't tell if Bella was serious or joking.

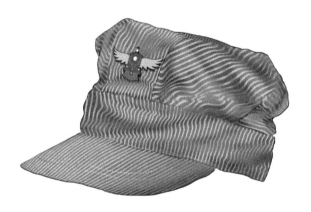

CHAPTER 13

Under the Dome

The tram ride to the telescope dome was scenic. Through a stand of hardwood trees, the three cars clicked and clacked past a pond with cattails and lily pads, and along a rocky stream. The source of the stream was a hill, and before reaching the hill, the track split in two. After the split, each track entered a different arched tunnel cut into the hill.

Stopping at the junction, the umbrella-clothesline-flat car detached itself from the cars in front of it. The two cars with passengers went right, while the flat car went left.

Neither the tunnel nor the tram had any lighting. There was total darkness for a dozen clicks and clacks, until, automatically, the red stripes on Benny's engineer's cap began to glow. Benny reached up and took his cap off to examine its light source. While doing so, he touched the train engine emblem on the cap. A beam of bright white light shot out from it. The engineer's cap functioned as a hardhat with a light, just like the ones that underground miners wear.

Benny shined the beam on Bella and said, "I guess Hercules was thinking ahead!"

Bella replied, "I must admit to not thinking ahead. I should've grabbed an XL collar when I first came in. I forgot that the collar bulbs provide light when the tram enters the tunnel. They're dual-purpose."

Benny could see a half dozen bulbs bobbing around in the lead tram car. He aimed his light beam at the bulbs and saw a dozen eyes glowing back at him. Delighted with the spotlight Benny had shined on them, the fan-club dogs started whooping and hollering. Their revelry was drowned out by the tram's whistle as it exited the tunnel.

As the tram slowed, Benny looked up, wanting to see the telescope in the dome, but his view was blocked. The tram was coming to a stop under the station's overhanging roof. Looking sideways out of his canopy, Benny could see that they would disembark into a large park plaza.

Bella stepped off the tram first and said, "This is called the Plaza under the Dome."

Benny exited behind Bella and hurried out from under the overhang so he could gaze upwards. He couldn't believe his eyes. A gigantic jellyfish was floating above him. He was amazed by the sheer size of it. Then Benny's awe turned into horror. The jellyfish had swallowed Earth!

Benny's voice shook as he spoke. "What happened to Earth? Is everyone okay? Is my family okay? You didn't fly me here because Pup knew a jellyfish was going to gobble up Earth, did you?"

Pup was quicker than Bella to respond, "Well-well! Swell-swell!"

Bella followed up on Pup's response. "All's well on Earth. What you see here in the telescope is an image of Earth projected by the star closest to it, your sun."

"The giant jellyfish is a telescope? I've never seen anything like it on Earth."

Benny had set himself up for Bella's reply, "Well, you're not on Earth, are you?"

Relieved, Benny now studied the telescope image more closely. Instead of a black void, the blue Earth was suspended in a swirl of reds and oranges. The sun's light was moving away from Europe and beginning to touch the east coast of the United States.

Bella explained more. "The telescope looks like a jellyfish, but it's really more of a floating eye. It sees what the sun sees. The red and orange swirls are sunbeams reflecting off Earth's atmosphere. What look like jellyfish tentacles are telescope connector cables."

Lowering his head, Benny tracked the tentacles down to a round platform that encircled the central plaza. Hundreds of helmeted dogs were lounging around on a raised platform, cables connected to their helmets. The dogs in Benny's fan club were scampering up a ramp onto the platform.

Benny watched as a half dozen colorful tentacles came to life to stalk their quarry. A yellow tentacle detected the mastiff's helmet, rippled around other tentacles, and latched onto the helmet's horseshoe magnet. Soon, the cables had all linked up with counterpart helmets.

Bella pointed out what Benny had already figured out. "The horseshoe magnet attracts a compatible cable."

Pup gave Bella a gentle reminder.

"Tell-tell. Smell-smell."

Bella picked up on Pup's cue.

"Pup wants me to tell you that the helmet allows a dog to do more than just see back home. The telescope detects odors, as well as light! Instead of a telescope, Pup calls the device a 'smelloscope.' Dogs enjoy site smelling as much as sightseeing."

Having fully recovered from the shock of seeing the Earth in the belly of a jellyfish, Benny raised his eyes again, wanting to better gauge the size of the telescope. He was trying to figure out just how big it was when Bella saved him the trouble.

"The telescope is 1,680 feet in diameter. That's almost a third of a mile."

"If the telescope is that big," Benny speculated, "the dome must be almost a mile across."

Bella confirmed Benny's estimate. "There's a mathematical relationship between the dome and its telescope. The dome is precisely one mile in diameter, while the telescope is one mile in circumference. The telescope floats in the center of the dome exactly 1,320 feet up."

Benny tilted his head back yet again, this time to check on what 1,320 feet up looked like.

When he saw Earth, Benny forgot why he'd looked up. Earth was beautiful, still blue in a sea of sunset colors. The sun's light had crept farther westward, over coastal North America, and was touching Florida.

Benny lowered his head, now wondering just where the telescope was aimed. "If the telescope gives the sun's view of Earth, is the telescope pointed at the sun, instead of Earth?"

"That's an excellent question!" Bella said with a wink of approval, the same wink previously given to Dyna. "The telescope points directly at the sun."

Having said this, Bella anticipated Benny's next question, "Now, you're going to ask me, how far away is the sun, right?"

Benny nodded his head. "Yes."

"That answer is tricky," Bella continued. "Dimensions and proportions are different here. Things can expand and shrink."

"Like things from Pup's pouch," Benny laughed.

"Like things from Pup's pouch," Bella chuckled in agreement. Then she went on to explain.

"A Star Realm mile isn't the same as an Earth mile. From where we stand here in the Observatory, the distance to the sun is the number π, backwards. That number starts with 3.14, but never ends. No one knows what it is, forwards or backwards. Whoever solves that equation will become as famous as Albert Einstein!"

Benny offered, "I betcha Pup knows the solution."

"If he does," Bella said, "I doubt he'll ever share it."

"Never-never, ever-ever," Pup confirmed, adding, "Walk-walk, talk-talk."

"Pup's has had enough talk of science," Bella said. "He wants to stroll along the pathway that loops around the plaza."

The length of a mile might have changed between the Earth realm and the Star Realm, but Pup hadn't changed a bit. Fun first! School second …

After a space ride, a carousel ride, and a tram ride, Benny thought a walk sounded nice. It also appealed to Max, whose wagging tail kept thumping against Benny's leg. Max loves his walks most of all! Benny knew that.

CHAPTER 14

Plowshares

Before setting off on their stroll, Bella made the same request every parent makes before heading out on a trip. "If anyone needs a bathroom break, now's the time."

Off to the right of the loop path was a "convenience area." Scattered on a well-kept lawn, among a stand of trees, were dozens of red fire hydrants. A blue-helmeted Chihuahua had opted for a bathroom break, instead of heading immediately up to the telescope viewing platform. The dog was tiny compared to the hydrant.

"At one time, we installed smaller hydrants for the smaller dogs, but they never used them," Bella said. "All the dogs, no matter what their size, prefer standard-sized hydrants. They like their authenticity."

Benny didn't know what "authenticity" meant, but decided not to ask Bella about it. It was a question he could save for Dad or Mom later.

Bella continued on the loop walk, and soon, instead of hydrants scattered among the trees, there were pedestals with bowls on them. Unlike the hydrants, the bowl-topped pedestals were all different colors and sizes. Benny's best guess was that the bowls on the pedestals were for water, but he wasn't about to commit to that. Things here were not always what they appeared to be at first.

Benny's hesitation proved wise. Bella stopped at a most peculiar sign along the walkway. The sign had animals pictured on it: a yellow chicken; a blue fish; a red cow; a pink pig; an orange turkey; and a gold stalk of wheat.

"This is the food court. There's a good variety of food choices here," Bella said.

With Bella's information, Benny figured things out quickly. The bowl-topped pedestals were food dispensers, and its color indicated the kind of food dispensed: yellow, chicken; blue, fish; red, beef; pink, pork; orange, turkey; and gold, wheat.

Bella and her entourage set off again around the pathway. The stroll took them past a crystal-clear pond where several dogs were lying on the pond's sandy beach, napping.

Pointing to a device that was set up near the beach, Bella explained, "That's an automatic ball-tosser. It can fling a ball one hundred yards out into the pond. I think the beach dogs wore themselves out."

Just after the pond, Benny caught sight of the flat car with the umbrella clothesline, the same one that had disconnected from the tram and taken the other track. The clothesline was no longer empty. Instead, there were several colorful helmets hanging on it.

A conveyor belt ran up to a small crane positioned next to the flat car. The crane had an operator in a booth exactly like Hercules' booth. Benny watched as a green S helmet rattled toward the booth on a conveyor belt. The operator manipulated the claw, lifted the helmet off the belt, and hung it on the umbrella rack.

Bella confirmed what Benny suspected. "The helmets on the rack are headed back to Hercules to restock his carousel."

Benny could hear a "click" when the helmet attached to the rack. He was certain that the "click" was the horseshoe magnet latching onto the line strung on the umbrella rack. That line had to be metal rather than twine or rope.

"The crane operator is Antares," Bella said. "He's a German Shepherd. He's bilingual like Paco. He speaks both English and German. But he's not very talkative in either language. He's a quiet, serious dog. Whatever you do, don't try to pet him. You'll lose a finger. And don't talk to him in 'kissy-kissy' talk. You'll lose a tongue. Still, I want to introduce you to him. It would be disrespectful if I didn't. Oh, and one more thing. I almost forgot. Antares is missing his right paw. There's no need for you to comment on that. He's very aware of it!"

Benny assured Bella, "I'll be very respectful and careful about what I say. I'll say nothing about the paw."

Before Bella could shout acknowledgment ahead to Antares, Antares noticed the group. He spoke in perfect English, "Hello, Bella and Pup. What brings you this way?"

"I was giving Benny here a tour of the Observatory, and we were passing by. I thought it rude if I didn't introduce him and his dog, Max, to you."

Antares studied Benny, then remarked, "It's always nice to meet a fellow engineer."

Benny didn't want to give Antares the wrong impression. "I'm not an engineer yet. I want to be one, but I still have lots to learn. Hercules gave me this engineer's cap as a souvenir."

Antares replied, "Hercules does not give out caps on a whim. If Hercules gave you a cap, you'll be an engineer someday. So, I'll say, it's nice to meet a future engineer."

Antares wore an engineer's cap identical to Benny's, except Antares' cap had two pins on it, one was a small purple heart and the other was a small bronze star. Benny heeded Bella's advice and didn't ask about them, knowing the purple heart medal was given to soldiers injured in war.

Instead, Benny talked about engineering. "When I'm an engineer, I want to invent a train that floats like Hercules' carousel. We don't have such things on Earth yet. My floating trains won't use gas or oil, so they won't pollute Earth's atmosphere. I want to invent special contact lenses for dogs, so they can see green and red. I think Pup's doggles are too bulky for most dogs to wear."

Benny had never told anyone about wanting to create wonderful new machines and was surprised he was telling this to Antares, a dog Bella warned wasn't very sociable. Benny felt at ease with Antares, a shared identity. They were both engineers!

Antares must have felt the same kinship as he spoke to Benny in a fatherly tone. "A floating train is a grand idea, but engineers must be practical. Your project is massive and requires raw materials beyond what Earth has available. The contact lenses for dogs are an excellent idea, and more realistic."

Antares turned to Pup. "I have to agree with Benny, Pup. Doggles are awkward to wear. They're good for enhancing vision in combat, but now I rarely wear them. Only on the Fourth of July."

Benny, too, didn't mind Antares criticizing the impracticality of building a floating train. Antares was treating Benny as a fellow engineer, and engineers had to consider limitations.

Benny responded to Antares, "I thought about not having enough materials to build the trains too. But Bella told me the story of how Orion turned Beatrix's harp into a bow. That story holds a solution. If you can turn a harp into a bow, you can turn a bow into a harp. All the materials that go into warplanes, tanks, ships, bombs, and missiles can be converted for the floating trains."

Benny seemed to catch Antares off guard. Silent and lost in thought, Antares finally said to himself, "And they shall beat their swords into plowshares."

Antares then apologized to Benny. "Please excuse me. I was talking to myself. It's a verse from the Bible. It means exactly what you just said. A sword can be re-formed into a plow for farming."

Still considering Benny's reply, Antares addressed Bella. "Swords are power, and I can't imagine those holding them ever giving them up."

Bella offered a different perspective. "And yet, Benny imagines otherwise. So, there's hope."

An orange L helmet and a yellow XL arrived on the conveyor belt.

"I need to get back to restocking helmets," Antares said, as he refocused on his work.

As Antares swung the crane to grab the orange helmet, he said to Benny, "It was nice meeting you and Max. You've given me something to think about, so I thank you for that."

Clicking the orange helmet onto the metal line, Antares swung the crane back for the yellow.

"I think the XL might fit me," Benny said to Bella. "Can I try it?"

"That can't be done. The helmets are only suited to a dog's brain."

Having said that, Bella made a different offer.

"There's a special device here that I was going to skip showing you," Bella said. "But now, I've changed my mind. I think you should see it. Although it might be more accurate to say it may see you. It's called a teleposcope, instead of a telescope, because it's telepathic. It views the mind, the world that exists within ourselves."

Bella left the loop path and headed toward the Plaza's center. There was no path to follow, so Bella created her own, zigzagging around trees and large rocks. All followed behind her.

CHAPTER 15

The Dark Corner

At the center of the park plaza, the very heart of the Observatory, there was a round fountain. Bella approached the fountain, Pup still perched on her back. Benny and Max followed. A mist of water drifted from the fountain and mixed with light beams streaming down from the dome above. The mist and light combined to create a rainbow arch. The rainbow was brighter than any desert rainbow Benny had ever seen, and desert rainbows were the brightest on Earth.

Bella walked through the arch, not giving the rainbow a second thought. Instead of following, Benny stopped to admire the colors. "Have you ever seen anything like this, Maxie? It's almost like you can touch it."

Benny reached into the rainbow and his hand disappeared into the violet bottom band of the arch. Max licked the band. When it proved flavorless, he snapped at it like it was a bubble. Pulling his hand out with no consequence, Benny stuck his head into it. All was violet.

Benny heard Bella's muffled voice, "Please pull your head out of there."

Bella and Pup had come back to retrieve him and Max.

"And whatever you do, don't step in," Bella warned. "If you do, there's a good chance you'll never find your way out."

Benny pulled his head out to see Pup frowning at him. Pup's ears were crossed in a manner that was perfectly clear: "That's a no-no."

Bella nodded toward the arch and said to Benny, "You go first this time."

Benny went first, with Max at his side. His two chaperones were close on his heels.

As Benny passed under the arch, the rainbow faded to gray. It wasn't just the rainbow, everything was gray. Benny rubbed his eyes. Everything was still gray, as if the front side of the rainbow had robbed all the colors from its rear side. Only a white brick path stood out in the colorless surroundings. Bella took that path, and Benny stayed very close to her, not wanting to stray into the gray.

The white path ended at a dark corner of the park plaza.

Bewildered, questions swirled in Benny's head. How could the plaza even have a corner? Like the Observatory, it was perfectly round. How could the corner be dark? There were no walls or partitions to block the light. It must be some kind of optical illusion. Maybe a trick done with mirrors?

Benny was still trying to make sense of things when Bella approached the corner and stepped into the darkness. Pup was still balanced on Bella's back when she entered, only now he was backwards, facing Benny. Right before disappearing, Pup tossed Benny an XL collar, with a yellow leash attached.

After strapping the collar around Max's neck, Benny took one step forward. He stopped short of the darkness, gripping Max's leash even more tightly in his left hand. He felt the same jittery fear as the first time he stood on the jump ledge at the Creek Canyon swimming hole, staring down at the dark pool of water twelve feet below. No, Benny decided, this was much worse. It was terrifying.

If Max and I fall 9,157 feet, accelerating one mile per hour every ten feet, then when we hit bottom we'll be traveling... As Benny did the math in his head, the terror dissolved.

Loosening his grip on the leash, Benny took a deep breath. "Well, Max, if we get lost in there, at least we'll be lost together." Benny stepped into the dark unknown, Max at his side.

The unknown wasn't dark after all, but a softly lit room. The source of the light was a luminescent crystal orb that floated, untethered, in the air. The orb illuminated the only other object in the room. That object was a brown tube mounted on a stand. The tube reminded Benny of the cardboard ones from wrapping paper he and Paco used for sword fighting. However, Benny recognized the humble tube as being far more than a play sword. It was Galileo's first telescope!

Ms. Clark had a replica of Galileo's telescope in her classroom. This telescope looked just like it, except for one thing. Unlike the replica, which had a shiny brown plastic cover, this telescope had a well-worn brown leather wrapping. It was obviously very old. Benny's heart told him that the telescope in front of him was Galileo's original.

Benny was about to ask Bella about the telescope when the orb started glowing brighter and expanding. Max reacted, barking, so Benny pulled him closer. "It's okay, boy. It's just a big bubble. It can't hurt us."

Just before getting so bright that Benny would have to turn away, the white light in the orb separated into colors. The colors took on shapes. First, pink and orange blended together to form a sunburned face, with rugged lines etched into it. Next, a swirl of red became hair and a beard. Finally, blues, yellows, and greens decorated the beard with beads. The orb became a crystal ball, the head of a red-haired, red-bearded man inside of it.

The man must have had a body too, because two brawny hands appeared and rubbed his two groggy eyes. It was as if he were waking up. The eyes then peered outward, trying to adjust to viewing the world beyond his fishbowl.

Max was now baring his teeth, snarling and growling.

The man spoke, his beard beads rattling when he talked. "Well, hello, beautiful Bella! You are as radiant as ever. And mischievous Pup, you have not aged a day! And I see you've brought a friend and his handsome dog."

Falling quiet, Max lay down on all fours, his front paws crossed. His ears perked up attentively. Whoever the man in the bubble was, he was no threat. Max approved of him.

The man turned his full attention to Benny, squinting his now glowing green eyes into the thinnest of slits. Benny felt as if the eyes were trying to look inside him.

The man's squint broadened into wide-eyed recognition.

He spoke again, this time directly to Benny. "Benjamin! What a surprise! So much like myself when a young man. So much like a babe I once held in my hand."

Benny was baffled, clueless about how the man might know his name. He must've mistaken Benny for someone else. Benny glanced over to see that Bella shared his confusion, although Pup wasn't the least bit surprised.

Bella studied the man. "Hello, old friend. I haven't seen you since the Battle of Hillsborough. I trust you're doing well."

The man kept his gaze on Benny and chose to respond to him, rather than Bella.

"Bella is being coy. She tests me," he said. "She doubts I am who I am. I did not fight with her at the Battle of Hillsborough, but at the Battle of Hill's Bottom. Her ear still bears a scar from that battle. But her back legs, I'm glad to see, have mended well."

Bella appeared to be satisfied. The man had passed her test. "You know me well, beloved Chieftain. Doubt is in my nature! After so much time, it's wonderful to see you again."

Studying Benny ever more closely, the Chieftain responded to Bella.

"You and Pup have brought Benjamin here to view the globe. Well, you chose to test me, so I choose to test him. Fairness is in my nature!"

Having said this, the Chieftain addressed Benny. "My test of choice is a riddle. Solve my riddle, and you may view the globe."

Benny grew anxious. He wished Bella had never doubted the Chieftain's identity.

Bella knew Benny's anxiety was because of her skepticism. "You don't much like taking tests, do you?"

"I hate tests," Benny replied. "I'm not good at them, mostly because I'm a slow reader."

Benny's reply drew a disclosure from Pup. "Double-double. Trouble-trouble."

"Pup has trouble reading too," Bella explained. "When he reads, he sees every word twice, so it takes him twice as long to read a book."

"I don't see double words like Pup, I see scrambled words," Benny replied. "It takes a bit of time to unscramble the letters into a word."

Bella offered Benny some encouragement. "At least the Chieftain's not asking you to read his riddle."

Bella was right. As long as the Chieftain spoke the riddle, Benny would have time to figure out the answer. He still wondered—why are grown-ups always testing kids, anyway?

Benny took a deep breath to calm his nerves and waited for the riddle.

The Chieftain spoke. "When all is lost, what still may be found?"

At first, "nothing" came to Benny's mind: When all is lost, "nothing" can be found.

He didn't rush to give this answer because riddles are always tricky. Benny thought it wise to search his brain for a better answer. Then it struck him. He didn't have to search because the answer was already in his head.

When the Chieftain presented the riddle, Benny had crossed his fingers behind his back, hoping he'd know the answer. Now, he realized "hope" was the right answer: When all is lost, hope still can be found.

"Hope," Benny answered.

Pleased, the Chieftain confirmed Benny's response. "Hope is the answer. Never give up hope, even when all seems lost."

The Chieftain vanished from the crystal ball.

Benny asked Bella, "Was that Chieftain Orion?"

"I believe it was Orion," Bella answered. "I've never witnessed the globe conjure a human before, so this is a surprise to me. Orion always did say, 'If you're too old for surprises, you're too old!'"

Pup now prompted Benny with a tone of urgency. "Hope-hope. Scope-scope."

Pup was right. Benny should view the globe before Orion changed his mind. Benny unleashed Max and rolled the leash up around his hand. "Stay right here with Bella and Pup. Don't wander off."

Benny walked up to Galileo's telescope, pointed it at the globe, and looked inside.

Galileo's Telescope

CHAPTER 16

The Battle of Hill's Bottom

Holding the Galileo telescope with two hands, Benny shut his left eye and looked into the lens with his right. The crystal globe shone brightly in the lens. Again, the globe rapidly expanded. However, this time, instead of growing brighter, the globe got darker. There was no avoiding it. A black hole was going to swallow him. He braced for it, clutching Max's rolled-up leash with all his might.

Then, Benny was engulfed by darkness. After a few seconds, white specks appeared overhead. At first, Benny thought they were stars, thousands of them, until he realized the specks were falling. One fell cold upon his face. They were snowflakes! Benny was no longer viewing, but experiencing. He was in the globe, and what was in the globe was real.

Benny now stood in the middle of a snow-covered encampment at the bottom of a hill. As a full moon broke out from behind the clouds, reflecting off all the snow on the ground, it was more like twilight than night. Benny could now take a full measure of his situation. Paco, Dyna, Bella, and Pup were with him, but Max was not. Their encampment was under attack from an enemy holding the hilltop. All, including Benny, had taken up fighting positions in a semi-circle facing the hill, their backs to a raging bonfire. Their situation was dire.

"Compadres," Paco said in a resolute voice, "there's nowhere to retreat. We must make our stand here."

The camp's outer perimeter was being defended by Ms. Clark and her science class. Benny's classmates were all wearing heavy armor, like knights, and, with their lances, were trying to fend off attacking wolves. Most had been knocked over and were squirming on their backs in the snow. Instead of warriors, they looked like kids making snow angels. Ms. Clark ordered, "Fall back!" The few who remained standing, then obediently fell on their backs.

The fight Benny always feared was here. Paco was right. There was nowhere to retreat. Benny had ignited the bonfire, the signal for help. All he could do was wait. He watched the glowing embers climb into the night sky, hoping they'd reach high enough to be seen.

"Show no mercy!" The battle cry thundered down from the hilltop, where DJ stood next to his wolf-head banner. The moonlight reflected brightly off his wolf-skull helmet and chain-metal armor. Over his head, he was waving a long spear tipped with a black razor-sharp onyx-tiger tooth.

"Hades," DJ commanded, "attack with your goon-wolves. Slaughter them all!" The huge goon-wolf standing at the head of the formation must've been Hades. He thrust his black spear into the air and the goon-wolves went on the attack.

Spears in hand, the goons surged past the vanquished science-class knights and joined the wolves to press the assault against those around the bonfire. A spear flashed past Benny, the tip slicing his cheek. Benny could taste blood flowing into his mouth.

Out of the corner of his eye, Benny caught a glimpse of Paco chuckling. "That's gotta sting, mi amigo!" In his left hand, Paco held a round oak shield with two spears embedded in it.

All seemed lost. Then Bella put her curved tail into the fire. When she pulled it out, it was aflame.

"Paco, grab the handle. Take the saber," Bella implored. "Together! To battle!"

Paco reached for the handle on Bella's hip and pulled. The blade slid out, as if Paco was drawing it from its scabbard. The blade was glowing blue, the hottest color, while Paco's face was glowing more violet.

Paco attacked with the saber, cutting wolves down with lightning flashes of fire. Bella inflated herself, not with helium, but with courage! Bella flew past Paco, dodged three spears and sank her teeth into Hades. By sheer will, Bella lifted the heavy beast twenty-five feet into the air and dropped him.

Twenty-five feet wasn't high enough, as the snow padded Hades' impact. Hades bounced up, his black spear still in hand, and hurled it at Bella. The spear punched through her right ear. She yelped and fell to the ground, injured.

Paco fought furiously, but his sword drew its strength from Bella. With her tumble, the blade lost its spark. Paco ran toward where Bella lay in the snow. Hades was standing over her, his bloodied spear back in his hand. Snarling, the giant goon-wolf bared his long, vicious fangs, and cursed Bella. "How dare you, filthy fleabag, challenge me with your pitiful, puny teeth!"

Paco was in a desperate race for Bella's life. As Hades raised his spear over his head, Paco cranked his saber back. Just as the goon thrust downward, Paco whipped the saber forward, spinning it out of his hand. Hades crumbled down, his spear missing Bella, Paco's saber stuck in his side. Paco had won the race. His prize was twenty seconds. Now, coming straight for him was an onslaught of goon-wolves, enraged at having witnessed him strike down their captain.

Swordless, Paco prepared to fight the wolves with his bare fists. A spear cut across Paco's right arm. Another plunged into his left leg. Paco fell to the ground, awaiting the next stab, the one that would finish him off. It didn't come.

Instead, wolves began falling on the ground next to him, struck down by sharp projectiles. Dyna had bolted from her position next to Benny and charged forward to aid Bella and Paco. Pup was with her, his pouch opened. Pup was passing Dyna daggers just as fast as she could throw them. Dyna wasn't missing. Every throw a strike!

Along with the wolves, the goon-wolves began retreating in panic. Dyna advanced to where Bella and Paco lay on the ground. Bella was in bad shape. Her ear was bleeding and hips were awkwardly twisted.

"She's still alive, just dazed. I think her back legs are broken," Paco grimly told Dyna. "I don't think she can stand up, let alone walk."

Dyna tried to pick up Bella, with Pup helping as best he could. Paco couldn't help at all. His right arm hung limp at his side. With his left hand, Paco was trying to hold back blood from a deep puncture wound in his thigh. Dyna and Pup succeeded in moving Bella only a few feet.

With resignation in his voice, Paco urged Dyna, "You and Pup should fall back to the bonfire. The wolves fear the fire and won't go near it. You should reinforce Benny. I'll stay with Bella. I don't think I can walk, anyway."

Dyna and Pup's responses blended together into one emphatic, "NO WAY. NAY-NAY."

Even from his position back at the bonfire, Benny could hear DJ belittling his retreating troops, "Cowards! Afraid of a little girl and her puppy! You're pathetic."

Benny knew the battle was far from over. DJ had yet to call forward his most elite troops, the armored, long-clawed bears. DJ now gave that order. "Bears to the front. Finish them off. Cut them to bits."

Dozens of bears poured down from the hilltop, clad in helmets and armored chest plates.

DJ shouted to his panicked wolves. "Reinforcements are coming! Reform your ranks behind the bears." The wolves rallied behind the bears, relieved to find cover from Dyna's daggers. Following in the rear, DJ taunted Dyna, "You know what bears love to eat more than fish-eaters? Little rat girls! My bears will feast tonight."

The full force of DJ's army was bearing down on Dyna. Dyna tossed another dozen daggers, all bouncing harmlessly off the bear armor and leaving only dents. Out of daggers, Pup passed Dyna a spreading knife. Dyna would have to make her defiant last stand with a knife better suited to making a peanut butter and prickly pear jelly sandwich.

There was a rumbling howl that had been growing louder, and now the howling reached a fever pitch. A pack of hounds broke out of the darkness and charged past Benny, who was now all by himself at the bonfire. The lead hound was Max. Benny had never seen Max run faster, racing frantically to reach Dyna before DJ's bears got to her. But even Max's fastest was not fast enough. Benny judged the bear was a second ahead.

Max must have made the same calculation. Breaking his stride, Max drew his four long legs tightly together and launched himself into the air from thirty feet away. Max became a blur and smashed into the chest armor of a bear whose claws were inches from slicing Dyna to pieces. The bear was blown off its feet and tumbled into the wolves behind it, knocking them down like bowling pins.

Max's pack rushed full speed into the breach.

The hounds' charge turned the battlefield into chaos. Spears flew. The bears flared out their eight-inch razor claws and struck at the dogs, while the wolves and hounds snapped at each other with sharp teeth. The hounds fought bravely, but were no match for armored bears and spear-wielding goon-wolves. The hounds were beaten.

Max broke out from the melee and made a charge toward where DJ was watching the battle from a safe distance. Evading DJ's two goon-wolf bodyguards, Max lunged at him. With a swing of his spear, DJ knocked Max unconscious to the ground.

DJ grabbed Max by the tail and yelled ahead. "Hold off. I want to finish off this mangy mutt with the other stinking animals!" DJ dragged Max to where the bears and wolves had surrounded Dyna, Paco, Bella, and Pup. His troops parted to let him through the encirclement. DJ tossed Max next to where Paco and Bella lay bleeding on the ground.

Nearby, Dyna was still standing. She was being poked and prodded by the spears of the goon-wolves she'd humiliated, many still with daggers stuck in them. Seeing DJ toss Max, she shouted at him, "Benny's not afraid of you. He'll kick your butt!"

DJ walked over to Dyna, punched her in the stomach and kicked her legs out from under her. Dyna collapsed to the ground.

"Then why isn't he out here protecting you?" DJ sneered. "He's a coward! A scaredy rat!"

For Benny, the waiting was agony. It took every ounce of his willpower NOT to charge into the battlefield. Benny kept asking himself, where is he? What's keeping him? He wondered if something had gone wrong. Time was running out.

Finally, there was a nudge at Benny's right hand. It was Rigel. Rigel had trailed behind Max's pack, unable to keep the fast pace because of his old injury.

Rigel spoke in Orion's ancient language, "Here's your arrow." Benny understood him perfectly. Strapped to Rigel's back was a bow and a quiver that held just a single arrow.

This arrow was unlike any other. It was far more powerful. Its metal tip was forged with four razor-sharp blades, instead of the normal two. The blades were coated with flammable tar oil and the arrow had a hollowed-out metal shaft filled with explosive powder.

Benny had built the arrow himself. Never kidding himself about what a bully was capable of, he'd prepared for the worst. He pulled the arrow from its quiver, knowing he had no choice. The arrow was his last resort.

Its tip pointed up, Benny lifted the arrow over his head and twirled it in his fingers.

"Hurry. There's no time," Rigel urged in Orion's language. Benny not only understood Rigel's words, but the desperate tone behind them. "Why are you hesitating?"

"I'm not hesitating, I'm calculating," Benny replied. "The wind's tricky. I need quiet." Benny spoke in Orion's language, and in that language "I need quiet" and "be quiet" were the same word.

Rigel quietly got down on all fours to be out of Benny's way.

Clearing all thoughts from his mind, Benny now acted instinctively. He loaded the arrow quickly onto the bow, no easy task since the bow had two extra strings to launch the heavier arrow. Benny twisted around and put its tip into the bonfire. The tar-oiled arrowhead ignited.

In the distance, in the center of the encirclement, Benny saw the wolf-head banner being waved victoriously, high in the air. He heard DJ proclaiming the spiteful words stitched into the banner, "All to the Strong! Devour the Weak!" The wolves howled and bears roared approval when DJ flung Dyna down by her hair onto the ground next to the others. Drool dribbled out of their mouths. They were hungry for their feast.

"Benny, it's now or never," Rigel urged, unable to keep quiet any longer. "True heart. True aim." The arrow's tip was glowing blue. Benny drew back on the three strings, aimed, and loosed the arrow. The strings vibrated a three-note harmony as the arrow flew. The music ended in a piercing metallic screech as the hot arrowhead seared through DJ's chain-metal vest.

DJ stood stunned in disbelief. Hot gases hissed out from the puncture. The gases erupted like a volcano, sending molten metal shards whistling every which way. The bears' heavy armor offered no protection. The sizzling shrapnel struck their armor with such ferocity that it set off a chain reaction of molten metal eruptions.

Benny felt a blast of heat blow past his face. A terrible, empty feeling hit him inside. How could anyone ever survive such hellish flames? he wondered. His sister, his best friend, Bella and Pup, all lost in the inferno.

Then, Benny remembered Orion's words, "Never give up hope, even when all seems lost."

Benny turned to Rigel for that hope.

"If there's anything you can do, I beg you to do it now?" Benny spoke in Orion's language.

Rigel looked skyward and recited an ancient chant:

> *Oh, Shepherd, Dear,*
> *We implore you:*
> *Shine your light,*
> *Hold it high and bright,*
> *Lead our brave ones, safely,*
> *To our sight.*
> *Keep them near,*
> *Hold them dear,*
> *Return them to*
> *Their loved ones here.*

The explosions quieted into occasional hissing pops. A dense smoke hung over the battlefield. There was a horrible odor of rotten eggs.

As impossible as it seemed, Benny caught sight of shadows moving through the smoky haze. Two figures emerged. Dyna and Ms. Clark were carrying Bella. Dyna had her front and Ms. Clark had her hind. Paco was limping behind, holding his arm. Benny scanned hopefully for more shadows, but saw none. There was only a strange sound of clanging pots and pans, which grew louder.

Benny had no clue what the clanging might be, when a rag-tag formation of knights rattled out of the haze, their mangled, soot-coated armor casting no shadows. The clanging knights were followed by Max's hounds, many wounded and limping. The knights and hounds were marching proudly together.

Guiding the march through the thick smoke and steam was the shadowy shape of a shaggy dog. The dog was waving a long staff high in the air, with a blue and yellow banner streaming from it. At the top of the staff was a brilliant lantern that illuminated the banner's colors.

Benny rubbed his eyes to focus better on the shaggy shadow. But, in the instant this took, the shadow was gone. Most likely, it was never there, Benny thought, an illusion playing on his eyes from smoke, dust, and steam from the battlefield.

Max emerged last, the captured wolf-head banner clenched in his teeth.

Max dropped the wolf-head banner on the ground and gave out a howl.

His hound pack broke formation and tore the banner to shreds.

Dyna and Ms. Clark set Bella down gently next to where Benny was standing with Rigel.

Pup popped out of the folds on Bella's back and yelped, "Help-help. Heal-heal. Seal-seal."

Pup peeled off his patches. The patches were field bandages. Pup passed out the bandages to Rigel, Ms.

Clark, and the science students. Rigel tended to Bella and Paco, while Ms. Clark and her students skillfully applied field dressings to the injured hounds. Pup pulled an ice bag out of his pouch and gave it to Benny. Benny pressed the ice to Max's head.

The haze had now lifted completely, and Benny surveyed the battlefield. There was only scorched earth where snow had been. All that remained on the battlefield were shreds of the wolf-head banner. Other than that, it was as if the bully and his gang of thugs had never existed.

Benny pulled away from the telescope, disoriented and dizzy. He wasn't sure where he was or when he was. Suddenly, the dark corner vanished, erased by a flood of light. Galileo's telescope disappeared too.

Benny heard Bella's voice reassuring him. "It's okay, Benny. We're all back in the Observatory. The Hill's Bottom battle is over."

Either Bella had read his mind or watched the battle as it took place in the globe. She knew what Benny had experienced. "The teleposcope placed you in the Battle of Hill's Bottom, a battle fought long ago against goon-wolf cruelty. It was Orion's single arrow that turned the battle's tide."

"It felt so real. It felt like I was there," Benny said. "Why was I shooting the arrow and not Orion?"

Bella answered, "The teleposcope senses what's inside. It senses that you share Orion's courage and wisdom. Perhaps that's why Orion recognized you."

Benny had his doubts. "I'm not a warrior like Orion. I don't even like fighting. Dyna is more of a warrior than me. The teleposcope must be wrong."

Bella persisted. "The teleposcope is never wrong. Orion's courage is yours. Orion was much more than a warrior. He was a protector. A protector acts with wisdom and holds true to what's right, even in the face of great danger. Orion inspired others to do what's right. You have his spirit."

Pup had been listening the whole time and had the last words. "True-true, you-you."

CHAPTER 17

Tails of the Dog Park

When Benny exited the Observatory, he felt dizzy and disoriented again. The world outside seemed to be slowly spinning. Adjusting, Benny realized the spinning sensation wasn't imaginary. The Observatory was rotating slowly. It was one giant merry-go-round!

After about a minute, there was a mechanical click, just like Paco's back gate locking tightly in place. The rotation stopped. Benny had no landmarks to judge by, but guessed the Observatory had turned a full 360-degrees.

"We're exiting onto the second outdoor level," Bella explained. "I thought you would enjoy seeing this most of all, Benny."

Benny distinctly remembered that, when he first entered the Observatory, there was only one step up. He had taken that single step with Max at his side. Now, there were two steps down. The reflecting pool, the gazebo, and the vast field surrounding them were gone, replaced with an awesome dog park.

"A dog never comes to the Observatory without a stop at the park," Bella said.

Bella descended the two steps and led Benny and Max to an overlook, where a grand old oak tree shaded a bench. Pup had hopped off Bella's back and was following behind the group. He was walking backwards. Benny didn't ask why.

The overlook gave a good view of the entire park, which had every kind of dog play structure imaginable—ramps, slides, see-saws, tunnels, fences, and much more. There were thousands of dogs in the park.

Benny sat down on the bench and Max settled at his feet. Pup curled up on Benny's lap. Benny was petting Pup's head when he noticed the hourglass patch on his back had been flipped over. It was now more full than empty.

All were enjoying the rambunctious chaos when Bella remarked, "Have you ever seen so many different sizes and shapes?" Benny could tell Bella wasn't expecting an answer, and she continued with her thought.

"Such a variety, from Great Danes to dogs that almost fit into your hand."

Benny had a tidbit to share, "The world's smallest dog is a 'Palmeranian' named Milly. Milly weighs less than a pound and is under three inches tall."

"Wow, that is tiny, even for a Pom-er-a-ni-an." Bella pronounced "Pomeranian" slowly, by syllable, trying gently to nudge Benny toward the proper pronunciation of the word. Benny still heard "Palmeranian," convinced that was a most appropriate name for a dog that fits in the palm of the hand.

"Did you read about Milly in the Almanac of Earth Records?" Bella asked.

Benny was about to answer when suddenly a Frisbee hovered just over his head, followed by a white streak. The streak made a 180-degree spin and snatched the Frisbee in mid-air.

Pup exclaimed, "Jess-Jess, best-best. Fetch-fetch, catch-catch."

Excited by the athletics, Pup jumped off Benny's lap and darted onto the field, frantically barking, "Arf-arf, arf-arf! Yip-yip, yap-yap!"

Pup's yapping caught Jess' attention, and she whirled the Frisbee from her mouth toward Pup. The throw was too high, or Pup was too small. Either way, the Frisbee flew way over Pup's head.

Or so Benny thought.

Pup's right ear stretched high into the air and poked the Frisbee, holding it while it was still spinning. Pup juggled the spinning disc from his right ear to his left and tossed it to Benny, who was still sitting on the bench. Benny caught it and zipped it back to Jumpin' Jess. The fun was on!

The Frisbee made ten circuits before Jess' eleventh throw spun off Pup's ear and tumbled to the ground, landing upside down. Pup cried out, "Uh-oh, uh-oh! Oh-no, oh-no!" and collapsed next to the Frisbee.

Humiliated, Pup bent his ears over his eyes. It was a good thing too, as Pup didn't have to witness the glare of disappointment Jess had shot at him. Benny had blown a point-blank goal shot in a youth league soccer game last year, so he sympathized with Pup's sick feeling of shame. Still, Benny had to give himself a mental pat on the back. He'd handled his miss far more gracefully than Pup.

Jess trotted over to the fallen Frisbee, picked it up, and headed off into the field. Her time playing with amateurs was over.

Pup returned to the bench, his ears perked back up, and the Frisbee incident already forgotten. As Pup settled back into Benny's lap, Bella said, "You know, tomorrow is a big day here in the Star Realm. Tomorrow is the Around-the-Moon Race."

Benny had never heard of the Around-the-Moon Race, so Bella explained. "Each year, in the winter, when my home star is closest to your moon, we have a race starting at Mars, looping around the Moon, and heading back to Earth's northern horizon. The dark side of the Moon is very tricky. It's an agility course with jumps and slaloms. Being the fastest doesn't matter. The dogs must be able to stop on a dime and head in another direction in a flash. If they go too fast, they'll fly off the course or miss an obstacle. Either way, they're disqualified."

This sounded very exciting to Benny, who wanted to know, "Are you in the race? Is Max? Max is very fast, and agile too."

"I'm not in the race. Rigel and I are judges," Bella answered. "Max is in the race, and there's a story behind his entry. Usually, only specialty dogs qualify for the race. Dogs with exceptional speed and agility.

Greyhounds and windhounds are the fastest dogs. Border collies are the most agile dogs. Max is a family dog, with no special training. It's rare for a family dog to qualify."

Benny was now even more excited. "Does Max have a chance at beating the dogs with special skills? Can I come back tomorrow to watch?"

"All the qualifying dogs have a chance to win," Bella responded, "but Max is a longshot. He's the underdog. No family dog has ever won the race. A silken windhound named Capella is the favorite. She's won four years in a row. She has a beautiful sleek shape and silk coat that allows her to slip through the air. Jumpin' Jess, the Frisbee-dog, has a good chance. She's fast, agile, and can jump."

"Whoops-whoops, splash-splash." Pup was still in Benny's lap, listening.

"Pup wants me to tell you about the new obstacle. This year's course is the most difficult we've ever had. We've added a final jump over a twelve-foot wall, with pools of water on both sides. The pool on the approach is very deep. The jump must be started before reaching it. The pool on the other side is shallow. If a dog fails to clear the rear pool, it can recover, but will be soaked. A dog with wiry hair, like Max, dries more quickly than a dog with long hair, like Capella. It will be a most interesting race this year."

Bella let more time pass for Benny to enjoy watching the dogs at play. Their unbounded joy prompted Benny to ask, "Is the Star Realm dog heaven? Will Max be here forever?"

Benny expected Bella to answer with a question, as she so often did, and he was halfway right. "This isn't dog heaven. How could it be? Something is missing."

Benny knew immediately what Bella meant. "People are missing."

"Someday all the dogs here will reunite with their people, Max included." That was Bella's full answer.

Benny sensed time was up, when Pup climbed from Benny's lap onto Bella's back. Max stood up and again licked Benny on the face. Bella hadn't answered Benny's question about coming back tomorrow to watch the race, so he asked again.

Smiling, Bella answered. "There's no need to come back. The race is visible from Earth for those who look up at the exact right moment. Where you live in the desert, the race will occur at 7:22 in the evening. That's exactly when the Moon will be closest to my star."

Benny had one last question and it took all of his strength to ask it without showing a single tear. "Will I ever see you again?"

This time it was Bella who couldn't hold back tears. "Pup will keep an eye out for you until the time comes when you're reunited with Max. Then, we'll see each other again. You must understand that my travel to Earth has limits. I can only travel in winter, when the Dog Star is in the night sky. Being on Earth drains my energy. I can only stay a short time."

Pup opened his pouch, took out a handkerchief, and wiped away Bella's tears.

Benny found himself comforting her. "You and Pup must always help those most in need. I will be fine from now on. I know, if I stand with my family and friends, I can beat back any bully."

Bella smiled at Benny. "It's time to say goodbye to Max. Pup and I need to get you on your way home."

Benny felt no sadness, only appreciation. Bella had been more than true to her word. Benny had spent hours with Max, not minutes.

Giving Max one last scratch on the head, Benny said, "You be a good boy. Don't give Bella any trouble. And, tell Rigel I said goodbye next time you see him."

Pointing to the playground, Benny added, "I've got to 'go-go.' You 'stay-stay' and 'play-play.'"

Max acknowledged Benny with a "woof-woof" and bounded off into the park, wagging his tail, in search of Jumpin' Jess.

CHAPTER 18

Steps Toward Home

Bella backtracked from the playground bench up two steps onto the Observatory's majestic portico. Pup wasn't on Bella's back, but trailing far behind. Again, Pup was walking backwards. Benny watched as Pup carefully placed each paw where he'd previously stepped when going to the playground.

"Why's Pup walking backwards?" Benny asked Bella.

Bella answered, "I can't even venture a guess. He does this every so often."

Not expecting any sensical answer, Benny took a chance and asked, "Pup, why are you walking backwards?"

Pup replied, "Back-track, back-track. Track-back, track-back."

Benny accepted he might never know if Pup was walking backwards just for the fun of it or because it was necessary to hold the universe together.

Once Pup had backed into place, Bella informed Benny about the steps they would take to get him back home. "The outside of the Observatory has five levels. You've already seen the first level. That's where we landed, and where the gazebo and reflecting pool are. We were just at level two, the playground level. You'll be leaving from level five. But before we go there, I need to stop at level three."

The Observatory started to spin again, and Benny decided to ask Bella about its rotation.

"Does the Observatory spin in a full circle? Does a step get added after each spin?"

Bella answered, "After a full spin in the clockwise direction, a step to a new level gets added. After a full spin in the counterclockwise direction, a step is taken away."

The Observatory was still in motion when Benny asked, "Just how long does a full turn take?"

Bella's response was surprising. "It takes no time at all. As the Observatory turns, time outside the portico is frozen. It's Pup's invention. A second is never wasted waiting for the next step."

Just then, the Observatory latched into place on level three. Bella hopped down the steps into the new level with Pup on her back. Benny caught up, and all three entered together into a planetarium. The room was dark, but its vast domed ceiling was lit with stars, planets, and a large crescent moon, which shined most brightly.

A gentle female voice called out from the darkness, "We're closed today, luvs. All dogs know this. If you're here to pinch a prime spot, I'll have none of it. You'll have to come back early tomorrow."

The light on Benny's engineering cap activated. He pointed its beam in the direction of the voice, illuminating a shaggy sheepdog. The dog was either gray with white markings, or white with gray markings. Benny couldn't decide which. The fur on the dog's head cascaded over its eyes so the dog couldn't see a thing. The dog's left eye had gray fur flopped over it, while her right had white. Benny supposed that working in a dark planetarium, sight wasn't so important.

"Essie, it's me, Bella," Bella announced. "I thought I'd stop by and check on things before the big race tomorrow. Are you ready for the madness?"

Essie shook her head vigorously to flip the fur out of her eyes. "Bella and Pup. Jolly good to see you. I thought you might drop by today. Everything's hunky-dory. Bee's knees. Blankets are spread out. Plenty of food and water. I'm ready for the howling horde."

"Benny, I'd like you to meet Essie," Bella said. "She's an English sheepdog. She's in charge of the planetarium. Every dog in the Star Realm will be here tomorrow to watch the Around-the-Moon Race. It'll be jam-packed. Essie shuts the planetarium down the day before the big event to get everything ready."

Essie raised her paw and Benny bent down and shook it.

"Essie, this is Benny," Bella continued the introduction. "Benny's from Earth. He's Max's person."

Essie shook her head in disbelief, her fur now flopped again in front of her eyes. "You mean 'Fast Max' who's in the race tomorrow?"

Bella answered, "Yes."

"It's wonderful to meet you, Benny," Essie said, her wide-open eyes visible again. "I'm cheering for Max tomorrow. Most dogs here are. Some dog needs to knock that diva Capella down a peg. Humble Max is just the lad to do it."

"And you thought you were the celebrity here!" Bella said to Benny, laughing.

Bella asked Essie, "Do you mind if Benny takes a peek inside at the night sky. He's leaving soon, so this is his only chance. He'll only be a minute."

"Any person of Max can linger as long as they like!" Essie answered.

His cap's beam pointing the way, Benny wandered deeper into the planetarium. There were blankets spread out on a perfectly manicured grass lawn. Among the patchwork of blankets, Benny's beam spotted water fountains and red and blue kibble dispensers. Beef and fish would be on the menu tomorrow.

Benny clicked his cap light off and looked up. The crescent moon was bright, but not so bright that it masked any of the stars. What shined above surpassed the star count on even the clearest, darkest desert night. Even more wondrous than the stars were the planets. They appeared closer. Venus and Mars looked like he could pluck them from the sky. Benny could make out the rings of Saturn and the storm spot on Jupiter.

Uranus and Neptune had such clarity, Benny could make out their colors too.

Benny was still looking up when Pup said, "Trick-trick, treat-treat."

"Pup wants me to tell you about 'All-Dogs-Howling-Night,'" Bella said, before elaborating on Pup's Driftling speak. "Just as all dogs come here to watch the 'Around-the-Moon' race, they all come again in October for 'Howling-Night.' If the sky is clear on a full moon night in October, dogs on Earth and dogs in the Star Realm can hear each other howl. I don't think even Pup knows why this phenomenon occurs. But it does."

Pup repeated, "Trick-trick, treat-treat."

After nodding to Pup, Bella added, "I didn't tell you everything Pup wanted me to. On 'All-Dogs-Howling-Night,' Pup fills his pouch with tricks and treats, and passes them out to the howling dogs. The dogs that howl loudest get the best treats. Grumpy dogs, who refuse to howl, get tricks. Pup will give them what looks like a delicious meat bone, but when they bite into it, it pops like a bubble."

"Max loves chasing down bubbles," said Benny. "You could blow ten bubbles into the air, and none would escape his chomp."

"Most dogs love popping bubbles," Bella agreed, "and that's the problem with Pup's trick. It ends up being a treat."

As Bella walked out of the planetarium, Pup up on her back, Benny decided to leave the light on his cap off and to walk out backwards. Since he'd be guiding his way out by looking up at the stars, it didn't really matter which way his eyes faced. Benny fixed his eyes on Bella's star and shuffled out.

As he was doing so, Essie shouted out, "Jolly good fun, eh, lad! Walking backwards in the dark. I taught Pup to walk backwards and navigate by the stars. He often walks backwards now just for the fun of it!" A mystery Benny was certain he'd take to his grave was solved. It was replaced by a new one, a mystery about dogs howling between realms on an October full-moon night.

Backing his last step out of the planetarium, Benny gave a hearty English-accented shout-out, "Cheerio," to Essie. It was the most English English word Benny knew.

Once out, the Observatory began its timeless spin down to level five. As the Observatory made its first turn, Benny asked Bella about Essie, "What's Essie's home star? She's so different from Rigel, Hercules, and Antares."

"Essie's home star is known in the Star Realm as the Shepherd's Star," Bella answered. "But on Earth it has different names. Some call it the Christmas Star. Some call it the Star of David. Some call it the Guiding Star. It's Essie's star that guided the Magi to Bethlehem."

Recalling his glimpse of the shadowy, shaggy dog who'd carried the yellow and blue banner, Benny asked Bella, "Was Essie at the Battle of Hill's Bottom?"

Bella gave one of her cryptic responses that left the answer up to the questioner, "Only if you believe she was."

Just then, the Observatory latched onto the fourth level. "We'll not be getting off here at all," Bella said, as the Observatory moved again. "This level is just for dogs. Pup built it. Dogs come here on their birthdays. They can choose any age they want to be for that day. It's Pup's birthday gift to them. Most dogs choose two or three years old and then head up to the playground level for the day."

When the Observatory began spinning again, Benny asked Bella, "What exactly is on level five?"

Bella answered, "I don't know all the specifics. From what I've been able to gather from Pup, it's amazing. I've yet to see it for myself. Pup's been rather secretive about the whole project. He's even given it a codename, *Granite Mountain.*

Just as Bella finished telling Benny what she knew, the Granite Mountain project clicked into place.

CHAPTER 19

Blast-off to the Bottom of the Sea

Along with Bella and Pup, Benny stepped into the fifth level, a cavernous chamber. A blue glow filtered down from above, reflecting off the chamber's pink walls. With each reflection, the glow changed shades, until it became a soft purple where Benny stood at the bottom. With his first few steps, Benny tested the chamber floor. The floor had a sandpaper texture similar to the Mrs. Bubbles and Mr. Juggles decals at the bottom of Benny's tub at home. There was no risk of slipping.

Benny walked over to the nearest wall and rubbed his thumb against it. It was cold and perfectly smooth. The wall was polished stone. Pup's codename now made sense: Some kind of specialized tunneling machine had carved out a geometrically perfect cylinder in a pink-granite mountain.

What didn't make any sense about the Granite Mountain project was the cylindrical chamber's blue ceiling. Whatever was above was not the sky, as it sloshed around like water. Benny could detect no visible barrier holding the water back.

"Wow! This is ingenious, Pup!" Bella exclaimed. "Balancing Earth's ocean waters against the Star Realm's helium to create a portal. This truly is an engineering marvel."

Benny was right! He detected no barrier above because there was no barrier. Helium pressure in the chamber was holding the water back!

Thrilled by her compliment, Pup bounced up and down, pointing both his ears toward the chamber's center, so Bella could fully appreciate the full magnitude of his Granite Mountain project. There, a colossal, glistening white rocket stood erect. The way back home was going to be nothing like the way there! The chamber was a rocket launch silo.

Pup exuded pride. "Boom-boom, zoom-zoom."

Benny quickly grasped exactly what hung above and exactly where Pup's rocket would "boom-boom, zoom-zoom" off to.

"Is that the bottom of the ocean above us? Is the way back to Earth through the bottom of the ocean in a rocket?" Benny wasn't so much asking his questions as expressing disbelief.

Nevertheless, Bella answered, "Not just back to Earth, but right back to your home. All water on Earth connects to the ocean, so once we get you into the ocean, you can travel wherever there's water."

Benny now gave a long, serious look at the rocket booster. A bubble was balanced high atop the rocket's silver needle-nose tip. It looked no sturdier than the ones exhaled by Mrs. Bubbles, the bathtub fish. The kind made by mixing dish soap and corn syrup with water. The kind Max loved to chomp on.

Staring at the bubble, Benny sought to confirm his suspicion. "So, I'm guessing the three of us are going to be launched in that flimsy bubble on top of that massive rocket into the bottom of the ocean."

"Oh no. Not the three of us," Bella answered. "Pup and I can't travel back with you. There's only room in the bubble pod for one."

Benny accepted his fate, as it made sense to him. Traveling home was a journey Benny needed to make on his own. Perhaps the last Star Realm test? Or perhaps a test of his own making? Benny couldn't decide. Test or not, Benny remained curious about his ride.

"How can such a fragile-looking pod withstand rocket lift-off, let alone punch through an interdimensional portal? And, I hope Pup considered how much water pressure there must be at the bottom of the ocean. Does he know about crush depth?"

Bella reassured Benny. "The pod's shell is made from pure hydrogen extracted from the center of Pup's star. The hydrogen has been bonded into an indestructible elastic material. The strength of the bubble's shell is not the problem."

"Not the problem?" Benny repeated. "What is the problem if it's not the bubble pod?"

"Gravitational force, g-force, is the problem. Once you punch through to the bottom of the ocean, you'll be swept up in a whirlpool. The spin exerts a force upwards of 10 Gs. Six Gs can be fatal. But, of course, Pup says he's devised a solution. It's just never been tested before. You'll be the first!"

Pup had already pulled his solution out of his pouch and laid it out on the ground. The solution was a zip-up plastic bag in the shape of a person. Benny hoped the bag was made of the same material as the bubble pod.

Benny wasn't crazy about being "the first," and wanted Bella to provide a bit more reassurance. "Even though I'm first, you know the suit is perfectly safe? It's a sure thing, right?"

"It's almost certainly a sure thing," Bella answered. "If something were to go disastrously wrong, I'm sure Pup will find a way to fix it."

Benny scratched his head in total confusion. He was familiar with "time loops" because he liked to watch sci-fi shows. Bella's rather non-reassuring reassurance made Benny wonder if he might not be caught in a time loop. Maybe he'd been smashed, crushed, squashed, and splattered a hundred times before, as Pup experimented to find a successful vehicle to get him home. In the sci-fi shows, those caught in the loops always found a way out. Benny was confident that, in time, Pup would find a solution for him too.

As Benny zipped himself into the plastic bag suit, Pup attached a small hose to a nozzle on it. The bag began to inflate, Benny felt like he was becoming one of those inflatable balloon characters at the Thanksgiving

Day parade. His feeling soon became reality. He was floating up in the air, and Bella and Pup were manipulating the ropes to guide him into the pod. Pup looked to be having fun flying Benny like a kite.

Benny yelled out, "Goodbye," but was certain the two dogs couldn't hear him. It didn't really matter, as Benny had already said his goodbyes.

Once inside the bubble pod, Benny looked down. Bella and Pup had released the tethers and were now scrambling around like a race car pit crew. Pup grabbed a hose and attached its nozzle to the rocket booster. The other end of the hose ran to a large cylindrical tank with the words "Liquified Helium" stenciled on it. Bella was standing at the tank, turning a large valve. The hose fattened as liquid helium flowed through it.

Benny could feel the booster rocket below rumble. A frozen mist poured off the booster, just as if Benny was sitting on a huge pillar of dry ice. The mist covered Bella and Pup, and Benny felt alone. He quickly shook off the feeling of loneliness, recalling the amazing adventure he'd had. He looked up at the ocean above, smiled to himself and thought—off into the wild blue yonder!

The rocket lifted off slowly, then accelerated at an incredible rate. Benny was compressed in his bag suit to the bottom of the bubble pod. So far, so good, Benny thought. He wasn't being crushed! In an instant, Benny was slammed to the top of the pod. It had impacted with the bottom of the ocean. The bag suit was holding, but the pressure inside was rising. Benny was certain he was seconds away from being crushed when the pressure dropped. He'd punched his way back to Earth!

The whirling started right away. Benny was pinned to the side of the pod, caught in an underwater tornado. He could feel the g-force increase with every spin, and wondered, if he had a g-force meter, what its reading would be. Along with the g-force pressure, Benny was becoming dizzy. He could take on even the spinniest ride at the Prickly Pear annual fair, but this spin was beyond any ride. He felt himself begin to black out and his last thought was—I guess I won't remember any of this when I wake up in my next time loop.

Benny came to. He was still in his pod, but now he was hanging upside down. He was dizzy and everything around him was white. The only place Benny was certain he wasn't was in a time loop. Time had moved ahead, but he just didn't know where he'd moved ahead to.

As Benny's head cleared, a blur of colors emerged out of the whiteness below him. The colors began to take on the shapes of sea creatures. The first creature to come into full focus was a long-tentacled jellyfish. This time Benny felt no panic, only amusement, even though the jellyfish was larger than the jellyfish that ate the Earth. Pup's playing a trick and it's not even "All-Dogs-Howling-Night," Benny thought.

Soon, the jellyfish was joined by a smiling giant sea turtle and a bulging-eyed, yellow- and green-striped tropical fish. The fish was blowing bubbles out of its mouth. This can't possibly be, Benny thought to himself. He recognized the two creatures. When a purple octopus wearing a red bow tie appeared, Benny realized what could not be ...was. Below was none other than Mr. Juggles with his colorful beach balls. Benny was hanging upside down, staring down at the bottom of his bathtub.

Bella had explained to Benny that measurements were different in the Star Realm than on Earth. Benny hadn't fully understood Bella. But now, being in a bubble the size of a pea, he did. Benny reassured himself that everything would be fine. After all, wasn't Pup a master of popping things to full size!

The drop that held Benny fell, but never reached the pot. Instead, the bubble pod drifted up out of the tub, down the hall, and into Benny's room. Suspended a foot over Benny's bed, the pod popped and Benny dropped, full size, into his bed. If Pup had planned the entire trip home, it was executed perfectly, except for one small hitch. Benny's head was at the foot of his bed. Completely exhausted, Benny sat up and flipped around. His head sank into his pillow and he instantly fell asleep.

CHAPTER 20

The Space Race

When Benny woke up in his bed on Monday morning, his head was still foggy from a deep sleep. As the fog cleared, Benny dismissed any thought that his nighttime adventure was merely a dream. He was certain it was real. It happened in real life. He was also certain no one, other than Paco and Dyna, would believe him if he were to tell them about it. Just then, Dyna came into his room. She'd been crying.

"Bella and Pup left! Pup woke me up last night and told me, 'Bella-Bella, Pup-Pup. Bye-bye, fly-fly. Varoom-varoom, zoom-zoom.'"

Benny consoled his little sister. "Don't worry, Bella and Pup are up with Max. They're all fine. Their world is wonderful, so you don't need to worry about them. They have an Observatory where dogs go to check on their people on Earth. Its telescope is amazing! It looks like a humongous jellyfish!"

Dyna's face brightened. "Look, there on your desk. Pup left me goggles!" Sure enough, on his desk were the pink goggles Dyna had worn on their trip to Alta

Vista. Next to the goggles sat Benny's engineer's cap from the Star Realm.

"He didn't leave you goggles, but a funny baseball cap instead," Dyna added.

Her goggles already on, Dyna tossed the cap to Benny, who was still in bed.

When Benny caught the cap, he noticed an embellishment. The cap had a pin on it. The pin had a depiction of a rainbow of colors converging behind the moon, and only a single color emerging and heading back the other way.

The pin was a reminder of something Benny needed no reminding of: The Around-the-Moon Race was tonight at 7:22pm.

Looking at the pin, Benny couldn't help notice the color of the single emerging streak. It matched Max's fur exactly. If Pup had left the pin, Benny thought, it was a good omen. Pup knows things.

Mom and Dad were extremely upset by the disappearance of the two dogs. After dropping off Benny and Dyna at school, instead of going straight to work, Dad drove all around the neighborhood for two hours hunting for Bella and Pup. Mom spent that time on the phone, calling the Prickly Pear police and the Animal Welfare Society to alert them to the missing dogs. She posted a message on Prickly Pear's town website asking everyone to be on the lookout for the dogs. There was nothing to be done but wait.

Back home from school that afternoon, Benny tried to convince his parents that the dogs were perfectly fine and that it was pointless to look for them. "You're not gonna find them here on Earth. It's out of the question," he told Dad.

The rest of the afternoon passed with no sign of the dogs. As the sun set and it grew colder outside, Mom even started crying. Benny reassured his parents that the dogs were fine. "I can even prove it. Come outside and look up at Mars at 7:22pm. That's exactly when the Around-the-Moon Race starts. Max is in it. You'll see."

Benny's parents saw no harm in going outside to view the stars. They reasoned that, if an imaginary star world could help Benny deal with the disappearance of Bella and Pup, that was a good thing.

"If we're going out to stargaze, I'll make a fire in the chiminea," Dad said. Almost every house in the desert town had a chiminea, an upright fire pit, on the backyard patio. As Dad headed out the back door, Benny raced out the front to go get Paco and Guapo.

When Benny returned, Dad already had the fire going. Mom and Dyna were standing near the chiminea to keep warm. Benny, Paco, and Guapo joined them. All were looking up at a clear, star-filled desert sky. It was 7:10pm, and a crescent moon had just risen.

Benny got a stick and poked the coals in the chiminea. He watched the sparks rise into the night sky.

Dad pointed up at the brightest star. "That's Sirius. It's also called the 'Dog Star.' It's a white star, but Earth's atmosphere acts as a prism and separates its light into varying colors, so it's sometimes nicknamed 'Rainbow Star.' That constellation in the sky next to the Dog Star is called Orion the Hunter."

Benny added to his dad's lesson. "Rigel is always at Orion's right hand. There's no more courageous dog than Rigel, except for Max. Orion is much more than a hunter. He is a protector."

The race start time drew closer, and Benny took Dyna's hand. "Watch now, over there, by Mars. It's the reddish-looking star, but it's really a planet. That's where the race starts."

Everyone turned toward Mars, as the clock struck 7:22pm. The entire night sky lit up with hundreds of silvery streaks shooting out from Mars, toward the newly risen crescent moon. "Those are the greyhounds," Benny exclaimed to Dyna. "They're the fastest, but the hard part is circling the moon." Some of the greyhounds were fading out and most were being passed by a silky streak.

"Here comes Capella," Benny announced. "If she wins, it will be the fifth year in a row." Two streaks followed behind Capella, racing neck and neck, a bright white one and a red one.

"There's Jess and Max," Benny cheered. "Jess is the best Frisbee-catcher ever!"

The two fastest greyhounds made it to the moon first and disappeared behind it. Benny waited for the greyhounds to swing back out, and when they didn't, Benny gave his verdict, "The greyhounds went too fast. They didn't make the turn and are probably tumbling into space!"

Next, Capella darted behind the moon, with Max fast on her heels. Jumpin' Jess was no longer a factor in the race. She'd veered off course and, instead of going behind the moon, had jumped over it. "That's a disqualification," Benny pointed out.

Benny held his breath, counting seconds: "One, two, three, four, five, six …" Capella emerged from behind the moon, but she was no longer a silky streak. She was wavering and shaking. Benny resumed his role as race commentator. "Capella must've fallen in the shallow pool at the last twelve-foot jump. She's trying to shake water out of her fur. Long, silky fur is a disadvantage when it's soaked!" Capella was regaining her speed, when red-streaking Max flew out from behind the moon. His acceleration past Capella was so great, the silken windhound lost her balance and tumbled down toward Earth.

Max raced back past Mars and off into Earth's northern horizon. Benny and Paco cheered together. Dyna was holding hands with Benny and Paco, jumping up and down, and shouting, "Go Max! Go Max! Max wins! Max wins!"

His parents stood there, speechless. Dumbfounded. They couldn't believe what they had just witnessed. After several minutes, Dad asked Mom, "How can a shooting star make a 180-degree turn?" Mom simply replied, "Well, Max was always very agile."

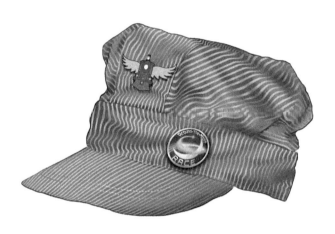

EPILOGUE

The Next Day

First thing Tuesday morning, Dad drove to the Animal Welfare Society. He told himself it was to double-check if Bella and Pup had been found, but he'd accepted that they were gone from this world. It really was a feeling from his childhood that drew him there, a sense that there was still magic in the world. After he asked if there had been any news about the two lost dogs, one of the Society staff members looked rather puzzled.

"No. Those two dogs you've been looking for haven't been found. There's something odd, though. Last night, a puppy showed up at the door. It has the strangest markings around his eyes. Almost like goggles. It has a single heart-shaped patch on its chest."

Benny's dad asked if he could see the puppy. When he picked it up, the puppy wildly wagged its curved tail in the air, like a cavalryman charging with a saber. Dad went home with the new pup.

Bella's Song

She dances into night,
the brightest Belle of the Ball,
She moves across the sky,
the moon lights her way.

See her step,
See her spin,
See her leap,
with pure delight.
Full moon night,
If it's clear,
You may even hear
… her call.

She plays among the Stars,
with countless friends, old & new,
And if they're so inclined,
a shooting star show for you.

See them race,
See them chase,
See them streak,
across the sky.
Moonless night,
if it's clear,
You may even see
… tails too.

– by Benny's Mom

The End

AUTHOR'S NOTE

John Ryan was my friend. A kind-hearted, steadfast friend. John died tragically when he was 13 years old. The life he had ahead was lost to this world. I have no doubt his spirit shines in the next.

ACKNOWLEDGEMENTS

Bella and Pup simply would never have come to life, if not for my wife, Laura, and my illustrator, Melissa Whitaker.

Laura has a magical way with words. She can make a clumsy paragraph vanish into thin air, then reappear as an elegant sentence. She can transform an awkward sentence with a turn of phrase. Dog Star Night is filled with her magic.

Most of all, though, Laura supported me through my frustrations and tantrums, as I doubted whether the story would ever be good enough to publish. It wouldn't have been without her.

When I was struggling most, I came across Melissa Whitaker's website, which featured her work with "concept art." At that point, that's exactly what Bella and Pup were — a concept. I couldn't visualize them. I emailed Melissa about my character concept, and she asked to read my manuscript. The story appealed to her. She'd once had a basset hound, like Bella. She now has a big-eared terrier, which was perfect for Pup.

Once I saw Melissa's first depiction of Bella and Pup, my doubts about publishing disappeared. I was certain the dog duo was as real as you and I.

My thanks also to Kelly and Lisa for their well-considered thoughts and encouragement throughout the whole endeavor.

ABOUT THE AUTHOR

Kenneth James has a rather unlikely background for the author of a kid's sci-fi fantasy adventure. For more than 30 years, he was a U.S. Defense Department intelligence analyst, a profession that demands the strictest adherence to structured technical writing. *Dog Star Night* is his debut storybook — decades of suppressed creative writing energy released!

James grew up in Tucson, Arizona. He graduated in 1978 from the University of Arizona with a BA in Russian Language. As a kid, he went sledding on snow-capped Mt. Lemmon, played soldier in the arroyos, and swam in Sabino Canyon waterholes. Even after decades on the East Coast, he keeps close his memories of the Sonoran Desert — the majestic Saguaro cactus, awesome sunsets, and dark, starlit night skies.

Now retired, he resides in Williamsburg, Virginia, with his wife, Laura, and their two 100-pound Labrador retrievers, Deemer and Pete. Together, they enjoy summers in their rustic summer cabin on the Coast of Maine, which James has come to appreciate as much as the desert.

ABOUT THE ILLUSTRATOR

Before deciding to dedicate her life to her art, Melissa Whitaker followed a traditional path. She went to college, got married, had two terrific kids, and made a career in real estate. Her art was always there, but it took a back seat to the demands of everyday life.

Then came a time when she knew she needed to devote herself full-time to her muse. Now, as a professional illustrator, artist, and photographer, Melissa offers vibrantly colorful and whimsical images with a sense of humor and wonder.

While Melissa began primarily with graphite and ink media, she now describes her work as a "juxtaposition of traditional and digital technology." She often paints with acrylic on canvas, photographs the painting, and imports the photo into a digital format in order to bend and manipulate it in a way that is not possible with traditional mediums. She is always looking to explore new techniques and evolve her style. In addition to authors, her work has been commissioned by restaurants, professional offices, daycares, and musicians.

Melissa currently lives in Oak Ridge, Missouri, with her husband and pup. She loves to hike in the woods and travel to other places to visit family, immerse herself in art museums, savor local food, and share her playfully ironic view of the world through social media. Her work can be found at Melissawhitakerart.com.

CPSIA information can be obtained
at www.ICGtesting.com
Printed in the USA
BVHW050414310522
638422BV00006B/138